DESERT CANYON

JEFFREY MILLER

The characters and events in this book are fictitious. Any similarity to real persons, living or dead, is coincidental and not intended by the author.

ISBN 979-8-9898839-2-9

First hardcover edition: January 2024

DEDICATION

This book is dedicated to my dad. He loved to read, especially mystery books. He would have gotten a kick out of his son publishing a book of his own. Miss you Dad!

1

As she slowly regained consciousness, a feeling of sheer terror and panic gripped her, and she struggled to breathe. It was as if she were being pulled underwater and suffocating. Her heart seemed as though it might explode inside her chest. It was completely dark except for some red light that she could see a foot or so in front of her face. Her head throbbed with pain and the back of her hair felt wet. She tried to move her arms but realized that her hands were bound tightly behind her back. Her ankles were secured in the same way. She was completely naked and there was plastic underneath her body. As she tried to move, she gagged on the fabric covering her mouth that was pulled taught and tied behind her head. She needed to calm herself and try to figure out what happened to her. She needed to find a way out.

She felt the sensation of movement and could hear some traffic sounds. She was in a moving vehicle. Maybe in the trunk of a car. She could smell the faint scent of a disinfectant in the air. Even though she was not wearing any clothing, she was sweating profusely from fear.

She struggled to remember what happened to her. She went to meet Lance after receiving his text asking her to come to the condo. She had been hesitant after the big fight they had when he caught her going through his "other" phone, the one that he never left lying around. She saw some messages from people that she didn't recognize discussing money that had something to do with the mayor. She could tell that they were discussing something illegal but didn't know exactly what it meant. But when Lance caught her, he became enraged. Did that have something to do with this? She was planning to tell him that she wasn't going to see him anymore. Did he find out her intentions?

None of this made any sense to her. Two men that she didn't know and never saw before were waiting for her at the condo when she arrived. They grabbed her and she tried to fight back, but she was quickly overpowered. That was all that she could remember before waking up in this dark place.

She tried to employ some of the breathing techniques that she learned as a child when she felt a panic attack coming on. She concentrated hard to relax her heart rate and breathing. Breathing with the gag in place made this difficult, and the fear of what might happen to her overwhelmed her senses. She was a well-conditioned athlete and normally had a low resting pulse rate near 43 beats per minute. At this moment, she felt like her heart was beating at a sustained rate closer to 200. She had to calm herself down and find a way to survive.

As her heart rate slowed, she began to gain some control over her fear and was able to begin looking for a means to escape. She thought there was some sort of trunk release on the inside of all cars as a safety mechanism in case a child was locked inside. Where would it be? But to activate it, she had to free her hands. That was proving extremely difficult, as the restraints were very tight. As she struggled mightily, she felt her skin scraped raw over the bones at her wrists.

Maybe there was another way. If she could somehow dislodge some wires and cause a taillight to go out, maybe the police would stop the car and she would be saved. She tried to contort her body in a way that would allow her to push her feet toward the rear of the trunk to try to locate some wires that she could attack. She was able to get her feet angled toward one corner of the trunk and used her toes to try and locate an exposed wire. The area at her feet seemed to be covered with hard plastic and thin carpeting. She pushed her feet and raked her toenails over the surface, hoping to find a fastening point that she could force open to expose the wires.

Just then, she felt the car slowing down as though it was leaving the highway. A short time later, the car came to a complete stop before turning and pulling away, accelerating again. She kept trying to free herself and find a way out, a way to save herself.

About ten minutes later, the car slowed and turned again. This time she could hear small stones being thrown against the underside of the vehicle. Were they on a dirt road somewhere? How long had she been in the car? She could be anywhere. How far did they take her from downtown Los Angeles? And what were they planning to do with her?

The car stopped. It was eerily silent for a few minutes. Her body tensed in fear, and she was filled with a sense of dread. Her throat was completely dry, and she tried not to make a sound, as if that might keep them from finding her. Then she heard both doors open, and the car suspension lifted as if two people got out. The trunk opened and she was immediately blinded by a very bright light. They cut the bindings around her ankles before they grabbed her by the arms and legs and yanked her out of the trunk. They threw her down on the ground and dust rose up. She thought about screaming but was terrified and didn't think she could even make a sound. And who would hear her out here in the middle of nowhere? It was cool and the air was still. The sweat covering her skin glistened in the moonlight. They stood her up and pushed her toward a small dirt path leading down from the road into a canyon. When they turned off the flashlight, she could still see the path because the sky was deep black, and the stars were brighter than any she had ever seen. There was no other light, just the moon and the stars. They pushed her forward gruffly but hardly spoke. They were large men and very strong. She was trying to determine if she should make a run for it. Just then, one of the men suddenly told her to stop. She did as he commanded, and then her world went black.

The discharge from the 9mm equipped with a suppressor rendered the two quick shots almost silent, as the small gunpowder cloud dispersed into the air releasing tiny particles of explosive material. The first round exploded into the rear of her skull before exiting below her right eye. The second round tore through the left side of her brain before exiting above her left eye. At close range to the back of her head, the first shot was most likely fatal, but they wanted to be thorough. They were paid to be thorough.

After impact, she fell limp onto her face with her body sliding forward and coming to rest in rocks and dirt at the base of some desert vegetation. They didn't touch the body or attempt to obscure it further from view, immediately turning and retracing their steps back to the vehicle. They got in and drove for a mile in silence without the headlights on, back toward the freeway. They had a few hours drive in front of them. A drive that would take them back to Las Vegas.

2

Sonny

He was up early, as was his practice. As far back as he could remember, he liked to be up before the sun rose to clear his mind and plan his day. And his day almost always started with a workout. Maybe the Marines were responsible for that when he was an impressionable teenager, he wasn't sure. But he loved the feeling that he experienced after physically exerting himself to begin the day.

He had a condo in Marina del Rey that afforded him a view to the west toward the ocean from his balcony. He bought the place after retiring from the NYPD and moving to LA to open his private investigation business in 2010. After the divorce, there wasn't much to keep him in New York. And besides, he always longed to live where the weather was more accommodating and ideal for being outside at all times of the year. The deep blue of the Pacific Ocean called him to make his way out west. He never regretted the move and loved living near the beach. The sunsets always made him feel connected to nature.

As he finished warming up with the sliding door open to his balcony, he thought about how much more important it was for him to stretch before and after a run since he passed the venerable age of 50. At 57, he still considered himself to be in his "early 40's" biologically but could still vividly recall the day he hit the half century mark. The big 5-0. He smiled at this as 5-0 was what the kids would yell down the street when he turned the corner in his undercover vehicle when he worked narcotics in the 90's. As he gazed above the green palm trees lining the street below, he could see the thick gray cloud bank settled in above the water. May Gray they called it. The onshore flow that Los Angeles experienced along the coastal areas in the morning with low, dense cloud cover. The difference, however, was that out here, those clouds would completely burn off by late morning and usher in blue skies and sunshine for the rest of the day. He liked the cloud cover early in the day as it helped with his running. A little built-in sun and heat protection can't hurt.

He was born Paul Anthony Romano in Jersey City, New Jersey in 1966. But all his friends called him Sonny. It was a nickname his mother had given him when he was 5-years old, and it just stuck. Growing up in Jersey City in the turbulent 70's and early 80's was a good way to learn the ropes, as his father often said. Raised in an Italian neighborhood, his father toiled as a local butcher and his mother was an elementary school teacher. He was out on the streets with his friends every day and knew the places to avoid. Race relations in Jersey City and Newark were not the best at the time, and he witnessed firsthand what discrimination looked like, in many cases by watching the police interact with black people. He knew that if he ever became a cop, he would treat people fairly, no matter the color of their skin. Law enforcement always appealed to him because he felt that it was such an important job, a job where you could really improve your community. It was a way to make a positive impact by giving victims a voice.

The time that he spent in the Marines in his late teens and early twenties really molded him. Sonny learned how Americans were viewed by other nations and how important it was to act not only with courage, but with restraint. He was one of the last 90 Marine Corps combat troops to leave West Beirut, Lebanon at the conclusion of the 22-month U.S. presence as a part of the multinational peacekeeping force. It was Sonny's first time outside of the country, a time of growth he would never forget. But it was this time in the military that truly cemented his goal to become a police officer upon the conclusion of his service.

There was a gentle breeze swaying the palm fronds as he stepped outside of his building and walked to the street. 59 degrees felt just fine. It would be in the upper 70's later today. He began to run north and worked his way over to West Washington Boulevard before turning west toward the beach. At this time of the day, even in LA with its ridiculous traffic, he could run on the street most of the way down without having to cross onto the sidewalk. He liked the feel of the asphalt under his feet as much as possible because it felt more forgiving than concrete.

Sonny turned right opposite the Venice Fishing Pier and headed north along the famed Venice Beach Boardwalk. Wide beach and the ocean were to his left and very expensive beachfront condos to his right as he progressed north. He usually chose to stay on the wider Ocean Front Walk for a while before veering over to the narrower concrete pathway along the sand. He did so because he never knew what he would see this time of the morning on Venice Beach. Actually, any time of day for that matter. Sonny knew the LAPD Sergeant that commanded the contingent of officers that patrolled the beach community. He helped clear several violent crimes by gathering information on the street and providing it to the LAPD. Most of the riffraff was passed out or just going to sleep at this hour, but there were some homeless folks beginning to move around, and vendors were staking out spots to set up their tables to sell their wares to the tourists that flocked here every day.

Venice Beach was an interesting place. Like most of California, there is a big discrepancy between the haves and the have nots. The homeless crisis in Los Angeles is only rivaled by that of San Francisco and Seattle on the west coast. There is a huge deficit of affordable housing all over California that is evident anytime you walk the streets or peruse real estate websites. The property prices in LA were not unlike New York City, but there seemed to be more options in NY for all different income levels. With the median home price hovering near $650,000, many Angelenos struggle to be able to afford a home and end up paying exorbitant apartment rental rates or are left to sleep in an RV or their car if they have one. The others are left to fend for themselves in sometimes violent tent cities in parks, under the freeways, or on skid row.

In Venice Beach, you have the contrast presented by the two million dollars plus homes along the canals a few blocks to the east, alongside the gritty beachfront area. The pristine beauty of the beige sand and water on one side, with the bright and colorful homes along the canals. And in between, it was the wild west. The homeless crisis is definitely more complex in a state with the world's 5th largest economy. Yet somehow, he couldn't help but think that should be an asset in solving it on some level. It was something that he had to get used to, as homelessness was handled in an entirely different way in New York City. In New York, you rarely had to step over homeless people on the sidewalk. The police moved them off the streets to shelters in large numbers. Here, even when neighbors complained that they were hesitant to take their children to some parks for fear of a mentally disturbed person accosting them or because of the squalid health conditions in some encampments, nothing really seemed to change.

As Sonny picked up his pace, his attention was focused on the black homeless woman who he saw most mornings. She was going through her possessions while sitting on the sidewalk, her trusty pit bull terrier always at her side. She looked to be about 60 years old, but was probably only in her mid 40's. Her hair was matted into the side of her head, and she was missing most of her front teeth. She and her dog had each other, so he guessed that was something.

Sonny crossed over to the beach side and things began to open up with unobstructed views of the sand and the ocean in the distance. The beach here was wide and deep. In California, it seemed like everyone worked out, so he fit right in. At 6' tall and 190 pounds of mostly muscle, he looked younger in some ways than he was. Sonny tried to eat healthy and get at least 7 hours of sleep every night. He always believed that he was given one body, and he was going to do everything possible to be as active as he could be for his entire life. It was essential in the Marines as well as in the NYPD. You see a lot of cops that let themselves go, he thought, but if you are ever faced with a life-or-death situation on the job, your level of fitness could be the difference between survival and being another name etched on a granite wall somewhere. Sonny also had an affinity for martial arts from the time his mother signed him up at a local karate studio when he was 13. Over the years he experimented with different styles, from Tae Kwon Do to Aikido and Jiu Jitsu. He was not a believer in the styles that focused on high kicks and other glamorous looking moves. As he grew older, he gravitated toward the more practical styles where direct strikes would quickly disable your foe.

After all, in confrontations on the street, you couldn't call a timeout to stretch first.

He was working up a good sweat as he approached the Santa Monica Pier. Sonny liked to run along the path under the pier before turning around and heading back toward home. He did 6 miles 3-times a week and paired that with some weight training and katas. Living alone and working for himself provided him with the ability to work things in at his convenience. Sometimes he would hike up Runyon Canyon at lunch time when he was in his office in Hollywood.

As he sped up to finish his 6-mile run, Sonny saw two LAPD officers cuffing a suspect next to a business along the boardwalk. A third officer rolled up on a 4-wheeler from the beach to see if they needed anything. Just another morning on the beach. As he cooled down and walked back to his condo, Sonny shifted his attention to what he would get accomplished in the office today. He had a few loose ends to tie up on a couple of investigations that he was almost finished with. Sonny stayed away from the divorce cases, as he didn't want any part of following errant husbands all over town. He was closing out a worker's comp case where the guy was posting all sorts of social media shots of himself surfing and hiking while simultaneously collecting workers comp for a total disability. The other was background for a prominent defense lawyer that wanted him to verify some of the information that police had gathered pertaining to his client's aberrant behavior involving a propensity to befriend young boys in chat rooms. It was Wednesday, so Francine would be in to answer phones and do some filing. She usually worked 3-days a week, and he would see if she had anything new for him to do. He would grab a quick shower and have a protein shake before heading to the office.

3

Sonny eased the gray Tesla Model 3 into traffic on his way to his office in West Hollywood. He decided to skip the Santa Monica Freeway and instead take a more direct path on surface streets through Culver City. The cloud cover was still dense, but he could start to see some signs of it thinning in a few spots with a hint of blue sky beginning to peek through.

As he drove along in traffic, Sonny wondered why public transportation never caught on out here. People seemed willing to spend inordinate amounts of time in their cars every day. In LA, it didn't really matter if it was rush hour, the traffic here was impossible to figure out. You could drive somewhere at 2 o'clock in the morning and be amazed by the gridlock you might encounter. Although most people don't know about it, LA does have a decent little subway system. It isn't anything like New York or some of the other transit systems in the northeast. It doesn't go everywhere, but if, say, you were in Hollywood and needed to get to Universal City, you could do it in 10-minutes instead of an hour in a car. He used it every chance that he got.

As Sonny made his way north on Crescent Heights Boulevard near Melrose, the traffic was very congested. He was watching some local street talent when he remembered that he should stop and grab some doughnuts for Francine before reaching the office. There was a place on Franklin that she liked, and he made a quick detour. There wasn't much of a line, so he was able to get in and out quickly.

His office was located on the second floor of a building along a side street a couple of blocks south of Sunset Boulevard. Nothing too fancy but it got the job done. Sonny had arranged for a couple of parking spots in the underground lot for Francine and him to use. Clients that came to visit normally parked along the street or in one of the small strip shopping plazas nearby if they could find a spot. He hustled up the stairs with his delivery in tow rather than waiting for the elevator from the garage.

Sonny opened the front door to the office and saw Francine seated behind the reception desk. "The Italian Stallion makes an appearance. Who would have guessed?" she remarked.

"I keep telling you, he was from Philly and I'm from New York. Two different places entirely," he replied.

Her smile brightened when she saw the pink box he pulled from behind his back. "Sonny, that was very sweet of you. Now I'm happy that I came in today," Francine said.

"It is my job to create an optimal work environment for all of my employees," he responded. Of course, she was his only employee and a part-time employee at that.

Francine worked full-time evenings at a local restaurant and used this job to supplement her income. When he advertised the position, he was underwhelmed by the caliber of applicants that applied. That was until he interviewed Francine. She was perfect. Smart, funny, and very attentive to detail at everything that she did. Just what he needed to keep the office tasks in line. She was a native west coaster, born and raised in the Seattle, Washington area in the small town of Gig Harbor. She moved to Los Angeles in her mid-twenties, drawn by the promise the City of Angels held for so many transplants who arrive each year to experience mind-numbing traffic, earthquakes, mud slides and wildfires. Somehow, all of that couldn't cancel out the vast improvement in weather when compared to the rainy and dreary Pacific Northwest.

After exchanging pleasantries and checking his messages, Sonny went into his office in the back and began the task of transposing his latest field notes to an investigative report he had started for the defense attorney who had retained him on a case the attorney had recently accepted. About 45-minutes later, the phone rang, and Francine interrupted him to tell him there was a Jim Summerlin on the line. The name was familiar, but he couldn't place where he had heard it before. "He says he is the Chairman at Sony Pictures," Francine interjected. That was it, he should have recognized it right away. "Put him through, I'll speak to him now," Sonny replied.

Francine transferred the call and Sonny picked-up on the second ring. "Mr. Summerlin, this is Sonny Romano. What can I do for you?" There was a short pause before Sonny heard a concerned voice on the other end of the line. "Mr. Romano, I was referred to you by one of our corporate attorneys. I need to speak with you in person right away if you can make the time to do so," Summerlin said. "We can meet in my office at Sony Pictures. Do you know where it is?"

"Yes, I can be there in about 30 minutes," Sonny responded. "Thank you, Mr. Romano. I will have my assistant clear you through the gate and have you escorted directly to my office," Summerlin said.

After terminating the call, Sonny closed out and secured the file he was working on before telling Francine that he would update her later on the nature of the request from Mr. Summerlin. In the meantime, he asked her to pull together a profile of Summerlin from public facing sources and the database programs they subscribed to and send it over to him via email.

Sonny left the parking garage and worked his way south toward South Fairfax on his way back down to Culver City. The GPS said it would take 24-minutes in traffic, but he knew that was always subject to change. While driving, he placed a call to a contact in corporate security at Paramount Studios where Summerlin worked before taking the promotion at Sony. Sonny wanted to get an idea of what type of guy Summerlin was, just a quick read. His contact, a former FBI Assistant Director out of the Los Angeles Field Office, said Summerlin was squared away and a decent guy to deal with. He was on his second marriage with no kids. Guys at this level were married to their jobs and that didn't always contribute to the best opportunity for a lasting marriage. Sonny thanked him for the time and clicked off the call.

4

Sonny arrived at the main gate a short time later and pulled up to the security checkpoint. As he envisioned, the entrance was framed by neatly trimmed shrubs and colorful flowers accenting the large gate structure announcing Sony Pictures Entertainment. After showing the uniformed guard his photo ID, the man handed him a bright red hang tag for his rearview mirror. He instructed Sonny to follow two guards on a golf cart who would show him where to park his car and escort him to the administrative offices.

Sonny parked his car and jumped in the passenger seat of the golf cart for the short ride over to the administrative offices. It was late morning, and the sun was now in full effect. The morning clouds were just a distant memory as the temperature climbed well into the upper 70's. He was walked through security and taken to a private elevator that carried him to the 6th floor C-suite. James Summerlin's office was located on one of the corners of the building with a pleasant view overlooking the studio lot. Mr. Summerlin's executive assistant greeted him and asked if she could get him a glass of water or some coffee. He politely declined, and she showed him in to meet Mr. Summerlin.

"I'm Jim Summerlin. Thank you for taking the time to come over to meet with me. My staff thinks very highly of you, and I need your help. Please have a seat."

Sonny shook hands with Summerlin and sat down on a tan leather sofa in a sitting area facing a wall of windows. There were large ornamental plants adorning different parts of the office. Mr. Summerlin sat down on a chair across from him on the other side of a large slate coffee table. "Please let me know how I might be of assistance," Sonny remarked, before waiting silently for Summerlin's response. As he did so, he studied the man. He was tall, about 6' 2" and about 220 lbs. with dark brown hair and brown eyes. He was in decent shape, but a little soft around the edges. He looked like a man that flew on private jets, stayed at posh resorts, and dined at fine restaurants around the world. He was impeccably dressed, as if ready to give a press conference at any moment or attend an entertainment gala. But Sonny detected stress and discomfort on his face and in his voice when he started to speak.

"My wife is missing," he began. "I was traveling for a 2-day business meeting in New York earlier this week, and when I returned to our home in Malibu around 8 p.m. Tuesday evening, Sharon wasn't there. I checked the garage, and her car was missing. There was no note or any text message letting me know where she might be. At first, I didn't think too much of it, but when I tried her mobile number, it went right to voicemail. I stayed up working on some documents until after midnight, but she still didn't come home. I tried her phone again, and it went straight to voicemail. I left her a message and sent her a text to call me right away, but never received any response. I tried the Find My iPhone app, but it didn't return a location for her phone. I checked our camera system, and it showed her leaving around 9:30 a.m. Monday morning, but not returning. I called the police, but they said there wasn't much they could do since she is an adult and not known to be in any danger. That's why I called you."

"When was the last time you saw her?"

"On Monday morning around 7 a.m. before my driver picked me up to go to the airport. She was still in bed but planned to play tennis with a girlfriend later in the morning."

"Did you speak to her later that day or on Tuesday before arriving back in LA?"

"No. I had a dinner meeting in New York that ran late and decided not to call when I got back to my hotel. I had to review some reports in preparation for an early morning meeting. I intended to try to call her after my meetings concluded on Tuesday afternoon before flying back but didn't have the chance."

"Has she ever stayed somewhere else instead of coming home?"

"No, not unless she is out of town or something. I work late and have dinner meetings several times a week. She usually dines out on the nights that I can't make it home for dinner."

"How long have you been married?"

"We have been married for seven years but don't have any children together. She is my second wife." He paused briefly before continuing. "She is everything to me. As you can probably imagine, my work is demanding and takes me away at times, but I don't know what I would do without her."

Summerlin stood and went over to a bookshelf behind his desk and retrieved a photo. It was taken at the Academy Awards on the red carpet a few years ago. It depicted a smiling couple dressed to the nines to attend the Oscars. Sharon had blond hair and blue eyes and appeared to be ten to fifteen years younger than her husband. She looked very fit and athletic in her designer gown, and her teeth were stunningly white.

"Please find her, Mr. Romano."

Sonny asked Mr. Summerlin to provide him with the following: a photo of just his wife, her mobile number, date of birth, social security number, the credit cards she normally used, the make, model, and registration of her car, the places she normally frequented, any scars, marks, or tattoos that she had, and the names and phone numbers of her closest friends to contact. He was assured that Mr. Summerlin's assistant would provide him with everything that he asked for.

In addition, Sonny asked if Sharon had any other phones or computers that she used. When Summerlin explained that she had a laptop that she used exclusively at home for email and web browsing, Sonny asked if it would be okay for a digital forensic analyst associate to drop by the home and image the hard drive. Summerlin agreed and Sonny said he would set it up for tomorrow evening. He also requested the email accounts she used and any passwords he was aware of. Summerlin gave Sonny the email account with Gmail and advised that she didn't use any other accounts. He also provided the password for her account.

"Thank you again for coming over on such short notice. I will call you right away if I hear from her, and please update me on what you learn. Call my assistant at this number and she will track me down," said Summerlin.

"I will do that," said Sonny. "One last thing," he continued. "Do you or your wife have any extramarital relationships that I should be aware of?"

"Absolutely not," replied Summerlin. "I certainly do not, and Sharon is not that type of person either."

"Thank you, Mr. Summerlin. I will be back in touch as soon as I have more information. I will leave my contact numbers with your assistant and send over a retainer agreement," Sonny said as he shook hands and headed for the outer office.

On his way back to the car, Sonny's thoughts turned to some of his own mistakes with his ex-wife Trish. He was so committed to his job as a detective that he didn't always see what was happening around him, especially in his relationship with her. It was almost a blind spot with him. Now that time had passed, his perspective of himself during their marriage had changed. Sonny now recognized that much of the divorce was his fault. He couldn't see it at the time, as it was happening. Kind of like being involved in a car crash. He wondered if Jim Summerlin was struggling with any similar regrets.

5

After leaving Sony Pictures, Sonny decided to stay on the west side instead of fighting the traffic to go back into the office. He called Francine and asked her to send over a standard retainer agreement to Mr. Summerlin's Executive Assistant. He filled her in on the basic details of his meeting at Sony Pictures and requested that she run a check on Sharon Summerlin to see what she could dig up for him to read when he got home later. First, he would take a ride up to Malibu to check the Malibu Tennis Club, and then see where they lived. Who knows, maybe Sharon would pull in the driveway while he was there, and the case would be solved.

Sonny made his way to the 10 Freeway, also known as the Santa Monica Freeway and headed west. The 10 came to an end at the Santa Monica Pier. If you took it east, you could literally drive from coast to coast, ending in Jacksonville, Florida. He flipped the visor down to cut some of the intense sunshine as he quickly accelerated and moved into the passing lane to get in front of a large truck that would have impaired his visibility. Since traffic was heavy, he decided to engage the Tesla's Autopilot feature and let the computer drive for a while. It was much more relaxing in the stop and go conditions he was experiencing.

In the meantime, Sonny placed a call to Detective Sergeant Tim Patrick at LAPD Robbery Homicide Division. Tim was a friend that he made while he was still on the job in New York and attended an advanced homicide investigation course at the FBI Academy in Quantico, Virginia. The two of them hit it off and spent some quality time running the dense trails on the Marine Corps base as well as shooting on the firing range. Tim was a first-rate detective and as a member of the elite Robbery Homicide Division, he had earned the respect of his peers. Because they shared a mutual connection as homicide investigators, Tim treated Sonny as if he were still on the job. After Sonny relocated to LA, they got together frequently to grab dinner or catch a Dodgers game, or just to talk shop.

"Robbery Homicide, Sergeant Patrick," said the voice on the other end of the line. "You working the phones? I thought you would be out solving crimes," replied Sonny. "I'm in here trying to catch-up on endless paperwork after we caught a double last night in North Hollywood," explained Patrick. "You remember the drill, I'm sure. Why don't you swing by, and you can bang a few reports out for us?" asked Patrick.

"Some days I wish that I still could. But this afternoon, I'm heading north on the PCH toward Malibu, enjoying my view of the Pacific Ocean," Sonny replied. Patrick asked what he was working on, and Sonny told him about the concerns raised by Jim Summerlin regarding his wife Sharon. Patrick checked the system and verified that they did receive a call from James Summerlin early this morning but didn't send a car after he explained the circumstances of his wife's absence.

"Wish we could do more for him but until we have something showing her to be endangered, our hands are tied," Patrick explained. Sonny understood and assured his friend that if he found anything indicating that she was in danger, he would reach back to him right away.

After hanging up, Sonny continued north toward Malibu, enjoying the scenery but wondering where Sharon Summerlin was, and why she hadn't checked-in with her husband since Monday.

A few minutes later Sonny parked in front of the Malibu Tennis Club. He got out and looked around before walking inside. Most people preferred to play tennis in the mornings before the heat of the day kicked-in, so the parking lot was reasonably sparse. The cars that were there looked like an episode of Jay Leno's Garage. Lots of expensive foreign sports cars with the tops down. Definitely upper crust, Sonny thought to himself.

After holding the door for a tall blond in a short white tennis dress, he walked inside and approached the young lady at the scheduling desk. Sonny introduced himself while displaying his ID. "Good afternoon. My name is Sonny Romano and I'm a private investigator working for Jim Summerlin. He and his wife Sharon are members of the club."

"Yes, I know Mr. and Mrs. Summerlin. They have been members for several years," replied the enthusiastic employee. Sonny explained that Mrs. Summerlin had not been seen since Monday morning, and while it was most likely nothing, he was trying to piece together where she may have visited that day. Sonny asked if she could check the scheduling log to determine if she had been there to play tennis on Monday morning.

"Let me check the book," she said as she consulted a large hard covered ledger next to the computer keyboard. "We have a new computer system, but our boss still wants us to make entries in here in pencil. He doesn't really trust computers."

"I guess your boss is old school," replied Sonny. "Yeah, something like that," she responded. Sonny was pretty sure that she didn't understand the reference. She found the entries for Monday and advised that Sharon Summerlin played with

Veronica Jones on court #6 from 10 a.m. until noon. Sonny checked his notes and saw Veronica Jones' name and number as one of the ones provided to him by Summerlin's assistant. He would follow-up with her shortly.

"Are there any additional entries for this week for Mrs. Summerlin?" She looked down again and turned the page once before advising that Sharon was scheduled for the same time today and Friday, but had not arrived to play this morning, according to the notes listed next to the court reservation entry. In fact, apparently her playing partner did arrive unaware that Sharon wouldn't be able to make it and ended up hitting with one of the Pros instead. Sonny thanked her and gave her one of his cards and asked that she call if Mrs. Summerlin stops by later this week.

Sonny got back into the car and entered the location of the Summerlin home into the large screen in the middle of the dash. As he drove off, he asked the car to dial the number he was provided for Veronica Jones. The call went to voicemail, and Sonny left a message asking her to call him regarding her friend, Sharon Summerlin.

Fifteen minutes later, he arrived at the Summerlin home. Sonny sat outside studying the neighborhood and looking for signs of cameras on nearby homes. The home across the street had a tall wall obscuring the residence from the street but had a camera mounted high aimed toward the street. It might provide a good view of any vehicles that approached or left the Summerlin's home. Mr. Summerlin told him that he checked their camera system, and it showed Sharon's car leaving around 9:30 a.m. on Monday before she was scheduled to play tennis at the club. He also said that she had not returned home since that time. He made a note to ask the neighbor to examine their cameras for anything that might have happened on the street that day if it became relevant to the investigation.

Sonny got out and walked toward the Summerlin home. It was a large home with a modern California design. The landscaping was very lush and provided a good deal of privacy from the street. There was also a wall behind the foliage that was pierced in the center by a gate equipped with an intercom and security cameras. He noticed a Latino man trimming a fruit tree and approached him.

"Buenas tardes senor. Habla usted Ingles?" Sonny said.

"Si, senor," replied the gardener.

Sonny introduced himself and asked if he came to the home each week and on which days. The man responded that he was there on Wednesdays, usually around 2 p.m. to trim the trees and shrubs. Another team took care of mowing the lawn every Friday afternoon. Sonny asked if he had any contact with Mrs. Summerlin, and the man said that she would say hello or wave to them when she was out by the pool, or when she was driving in her car and leaving or coming home. He had not seen her this week and didn't have anything else of substance to offer. Sonny thanked him and went back to his car. He would come back and canvass the neighbors if that became necessary. For now, he headed back to the PCH to drive south toward his condo to read the information that he asked Francine to send to him.

As he surrendered to the dense traffic on the PCH, Sonny was focused on the probabilities associated with Sharon failing to check in if she was not in danger. Just then, his phone rang, and the car display showed the number for Veronica Jones. While he would have preferred to speak to her face to face, he was trying to gather information quickly at this stage and would have the chance to meet with her and gauge her body language later.

"Sonny Romano," he said into the car's microphone after accepting the call. "This is Veronica Jones. You left me a message about Sharon," she replied. Sonny explained how he became involved in the case and asked her when she last spoke to her friend Sharon. Veronica confirmed that they had a tennis date on Monday morning from 10 o'clock a.m. until noon. They both spent time in the sauna before showering at the club. They then went in separate cars to do some shopping together in Beverly Hills before having a late lunch at Villa Blanca. They sat and talked for a while, as neither had any place they had to be, and left the restaurant around 4 p.m. That was the last time that she saw or spoke to Sharon.

"Is there something wrong? She didn't meet me for tennis this morning and she usually calls if she can't make it," Sharon said. "With you asking me these questions, I am starting to become concerned about her," she continued. "What did Jim say?"

"Jim has not heard from her since early on Monday morning. She has not been home since she left to play tennis with you the the club," Sonny responded. "Do you have any idea where she could have gone if she didn't go home?"

There was a pause before Veronica replied. "No, I really can't say where she might be," Veronica replied. Sonny was struck by the precise words that she chose to use in answering his question.

"I have to go now," she said. "I'm at my daughter's school and need to pick her up from practice."

Sonny thanked her and asked that she call him right away if she heard from Sharon by any means. He concluded by telling her that he may need to meet with her later at a convenient time for her to discuss any additional information that he gathers. "Okay, that would be fine," Veronica said before disconnecting the call.

Sonny was replaying the conversation in his mind as he drove south. She appeared legitimately concerned about what may have happened to her friend, but also seemed to be withholding something. She didn't know him, and they were speaking over the phone, but he was still considering her reply: *I can't really say where she might be.* As if she may know where she is but did not want to betray the confidence of her friend. If that was the case, perhaps Veronica believed that she could contact Sharon and confirm that she was okay. He would follow-up with Veronica tomorrow, in person if possible.

6

Jimmy and Frank (Monday, two days earlier)

Frank hung up the phone and told Jimmy that they had to go see the boss at the club. Jimmy wheeled the Cadillac around completely at the next intersection and headed back in the direction of the Las Vegas strip. The two men were dressed similarly, wearing untucked short sleeve shirts and dress slacks. It wasn't a small car, but they nearly bumped elbows sitting next to each other in the front seats. Both men weighed in the neighborhood of 300 pounds, with broad shoulders and thick necks. They also shared an affinity for gold chains and pinky rings.

As they approached Las Vegas Boulevard, Jimmy steered the car north a few blocks short of the strip down a side road leading past a golf course and several restaurants and businesses. They continued for several blocks before pulling into the parking lot of a restaurant and lounge called Frank's Place, but no relation to the man sitting in the passenger seat. The name was a salute to Frank Sinatra, from the time when the Rat Pack ruled Vegas. He pulled around to the back and parked in a handicapped spot near the rear employee entrance. The men entered and went through the kitchen and down a hallway past the bar and took a set of stairs right before the door leading to the restaurant portion of the establishment. The steps led to an office located on the second floor, tucked away from view. At the top of the steps, they encountered one of their colleagues, Sal, smoking a cigarette while leaning on a stool with a large handgun hanging upside down under his left arm. "He's waiting for you inside," Sal informed them. "He's not in a good mood."

They knocked on the door before opening it, awaiting the okay before stepping inside. The office was bare bones and bereft of art or personal photographs. The man sitting behind the large oak desk peered up over his reading glasses and told them to sit. They did as he commanded but did not speak and waited to be spoken to.

Antonio "Tony" Bianchi was not known for pleasantries. He was direct and to the point. "Our friend down south got sloppy. He made a mistake, and you need to go and clean it up. Call our friend at this number when you arrive, and he will provide what you need to get inside the condo and wait for the package. Take the package and dispose of it on your way back here. Be very careful and don't allow anything to touch me or you will be the next package we dispose of. Capisce?"

The men nodded and took an envelope he handed them containing a rental car reservation in the name of Richard Francis, along with a phony driver license in the same name containing Jimmy's photo. They would need to pick-up the rental in time to leave Vegas by 2 p.m. to get to Los Angeles around 6 p.m. or so. As they left the club, Frank looked at his watch and told Jimmy they would have time to grab lunch before heading south. The two men drove in silence on the way to a restaurant they liked to frequent, focused on the task ahead of them.

Six hours later, they parked the rental in a parking garage a few blocks from City Hall. There was a nice breeze that greeted them when they stepped onto the sidewalk. The afternoon sun was blocked by the taller buildings. Lance was supposed to be in a coffee shop just down the block from them. When they got closer, Frank saw him at a standing table near the window facing the street. Their eyes met, and Frank entered the establishment. Jimmy kept walking south toward the bus stop enclosure near the next intersection.

When Frank entered, he walked toward the restroom as if needing to wash his hands. When he came out, he passed by Lance and picked-up the small envelope protruding from the table next to Lance's right elbow and kept walking. No words were exchanged between the two as Frank walked back out the door and onto the sidewalk. Jimmy joined him and they strolled back toward the parking garage where they left the rental car.

7

Sonny was staring off into the distance before the dawn arrived, thinking about Sharon Summerlin and what might have become of her. He was worried about her because every trap he had run thus far suggested there was something amiss. Not enough to know with certainty that she was in danger, but as an experienced investigator, his gut told him this was trending in the wrong direction. He hoped that he was mistaken, and she would soon surface safely with an explanation that would account for her falling off the grid. Unfortunately, the passage of time was starting to make that outcome far less likely.

After calling Jim Summerlin last evening and filling him in on his actions from yesterday afternoon, Sonny placed a call to Sharon's parents in Texas to see what more he could learn about her. He then spent the evening pouring over the documents that Francine emailed to him. In doing so, he was able to develop a more detailed picture of Sharon's life. Afterward, Sonny felt almost as if he knew her at least in some small way. That may prove helpful as the investigation progressed.

Sharon was born in Dallas, Texas and raised in Fort Worth. She was an only child and her parents provided her with a loving home and all the support she needed to develop a strong sense of self confidence. She excelled in sports, earning a full scholarship in soccer to attend Baylor University where she studied psychology. However, it was an elective course in film study that sparked an interest in the motion picture industry that she never knew existed before. After college, she headed to

Hollywood and took an entry level position at Paramount Studios. After a few years, she had worked her way into the production side of the film industry while sharing an apartment with two roommates to make ends meet. It was at this time that she caught the attention of Jim Summerlin, then a rising star on the business side of Paramount. They met at a company function at one of the entertainment parks, and their chance encounter led to spending some time together outside of the studio. Jim was 15-years older than Sharon, but they apparently were a good match. They kept the relationship quiet since that type of thing was frowned upon by the HR department at Paramount. A few months later, Jim Summerlin left to accept a promotion at Sony Entertainment. Sharon continued to work in production at Paramount until they decided to get married. It was his second marriage and her first. After the wedding, she moved into his home in Malibu and began an entirely new life as the wife of a wealthy studio executive.

Sonny was weighing how such a stark change in personal circumstances might affect one's psyche when his mobile phone began to vibrate. He glanced at the clock next to his bed and saw that it was only 4:45 a.m. and a bit early for someone to call. Not completely unusual, especially if it was someone from the east coast, oblivious to the 3-hour time difference. He picked up the phone and saw that it was Tim Patrick and he braced for bad news.

"Tim, what's going on?" he answered.

"Sonny, I'm sorry to call this early but I knew you would want me to," Tim began. He went on to explain that he had placed a flag on Sharon Summerlin's drivers license and her vehicle registration files within LAPD's interface to the California DMV records system. This way, if someone at the LAPD ran her name or her vehicle registration through the computer via dispatch, the flag would pop up so the dispatcher could inform the inquiring officer to contact Sergeant Patrick at Robbery Homicide before taking further action.

"I received a call ten minutes ago that a patrol unit ran the registration number of Sharon Summerlin's vehicle in an underground parking garage at LA Live," Patrick outlined. He explained that the security team called it in to LAPD because the car had been parked there for a few days, and due to the value of the vehicle, it seemed suspicious.

"How quickly can you get down there?" Tim asked.

"I can be there within 30-minutes," Sonny responded.

"Okay, I will have the black and white stand by until you arrive and determine how you want to proceed." Tim clicked off and relayed the message through dispatch.

Sonny called Jim Summerlin and was surprised that he answered at this hour. He informed him of what he just learned and asked him to meet at the parking garage as soon as he could get there with an extra key to Sharon's car. Jim agreed and Sonny quickly got dressed and headed for LA Live.

At this hour of the morning, there was still a fair amount of traffic on the 10 Freeway heading east toward the Staple's Center. He took advantage of the Tesla's quick acceleration to pass slower traffic by switching between lanes, assuring that he would get there as soon as possible. It was still dark, but he could see the horizon brightening in front of him and daylight wouldn't be too far behind.

Sonny arrived at the underground parking garage precisely 26-minutes after hanging up with Tim Patrick. As he got out of his car, he observed one of the uniformed officers standing outside leaning against the patrol car's right front fender while the other officer was inside typing on the keyboard of the mobile computer. Probably trying to get a jump on some paperwork from earlier in the shift, Sonny thought to himself. A private security officer sat on a golf cart with a flashing yellow light a few spots away from the red 2020 Mercedes SL convertible registered to Sharon Summerlin.

"Was the car locked when you found it?" Sonny asked the officer who pushed off the fender and moved toward him. "Yes, locked and unattended," the officer replied. Sonny introduced himself and the officer confirmed that Sergeant Patrick asked them to stand by until he arrived. "We didn't touch anything, just looked inside through the windows to see if there was anything that seemed to be out of place," The officer informed him.

Sonny walked over to the car as he put on a pair of disposable gloves. He didn't want to disturb anything in case the vehicle would need to be processed by evidence technicians. He walked completely around the car examining the vehicle to see if anything about the wheels, tires or lower sidewalls exhibited something inconsistent with the current surroundings. The car was very clean, as if it had been washed in the last few days. The garage was well lit, and it seemed to be as bright as daylight, precluding the need for the small flashlight in his pocket. As Sonny peered through the windows, he saw that the interior was a tan colored leather and appeared to be very neat and clean. The only item that he could see was the parking receipt positioned upside down in the cup holder in the center console. He took out his phone and photographed the vehicle from several angles, as well as the interior through the windows.

"Does your camera system cover this portion of the garage with a clear view of this parking stall?" Sonny asked the security guard on the golf cart. "Yes, Sir," the man replied. "I can have the desk officer pull the footage showing when the vehicle arrived and who parked it, but you will have to get permission from our boss to view it," the guard declared. Sonny asked him when his boss arrives for work and learned that he wouldn't arrive until 8am. Since it was only 5:25 a.m. now, he would need to come back closer to 8 o'clock.

Just then a dark blue Porsche Panamera pulled into the garage and approached their position. Jim Summerlin parked and stepped out of his car and activated the key fob unlocking the doors to Sharon's car. "I got here as soon as I could," Jim advised. "Did you find anything?"

"So far, nothing looks out of place," replied Sonny. "I'd like to look through the interior and check the trunk," Sonny stated as he walked around to the driver's door while Jim Summerlin watched. He examined everything inside the car including looking under the seats and floor mats. He checked the glove box and center console. Still wearing gloves, he lifted the parking receipt out of the cup holder and looked at the time stamp. It showed that she entered the garage at 9:21 p.m. on Monday, May 4th, three days earlier. This should be able to be verified by the video. There was no trace of anything unusual inside the car or in the trunk. No mobile phone was left in the vehicle either.

While Sonny was searching the car and taking some additional photos, a dark colored SUV with tinted windows rolled up next to the Porsche. Two members of Jim's security detail had met him at the garage. One would drive Sharon's car back to their home and park it safely inside of their garage where it would not be disturbed just in case the police needed to process it later. The other would follow Jim in the SUV and they would wait for Jim to get changed for work and then take him to his office at Sony Pictures.

Sonny informed Jim that he was going to run over to his office but would come back at 8am to view the video. He wanted to determine if Sharon was the one that parked the car, whether she was alone, and if anyone followed her or met up with her inside the garage. He promised to call and let Jim know what he learned after watching the security video.

After Jim left with his security team, Sonny thanked the LAPD officers for their assistance and told the security guard to have the video queued up and to advise his boss to expect him at 8 a.m. sharp. He then got back into his car and headed for his office in Hollywood.

8

Mark and Susan Johnson were really looking forward to their vacation in beautiful Palm Springs, California. They had saved for the past year and meticulously planned their first trip to the Golden State. As avid hikers, they read about all the great hiking trails throughout the area and planned to explore several of them this week. After arriving on Wednesday night and checking in to their hotel with a fantastic view of the San Jacinto mountains, they could hardly control their excitement when they woke up early Thursday morning to hit the trails.

Since they were from the Midwest, they had no trouble waking up well before dawn. That was perfect, as it was advantageous to begin at first light on the east side of the mountain trail so they would be coming down the west facing side as the sun began to bake the Coachella Valley. This would at least afford some shade before the sun got too high in the sky. Even though it was early May, the temperatures were already climbing into the low triple digits most days. You didn't want to be the tourists that hadn't planned well and ventured out too late in the morning without adequate hydration, sunscreen, and a good GPS way finder. The Johnsons were equipped with all the proper gear, including the Camelbacks filled with water that each brought along to strap on their backs.

Mark pulled the rental car around to the lobby entrance and picked Susan up, and they set out for the trail head a few miles away. There was a small dirt parking area near the trail, large enough to accommodate several vehicles. They found the lot empty on this day at this early hour. As the weather began to heat up in the desert, the number of people thinned out significantly, leaving mostly hearty locals that enjoyed the decrease in visitors and traffic, and those seeking to take advantage of lower priced hotel rooms. Most of the wealthy people that owned property in the area had other homes to go back to during the summer months. Palm Springs was perfect about 9 months of the year but was known to reach temperatures in the low 120's during the summer months.

Mark and Susan strapped on their Camelbacks and began the ascent on the trail from the east as the sun began to peek over the horizon. There was no wind, and the conditions were perfect. They couldn't wait to see the view of the desert floor from the highest point on the trail. Their pulses began to accelerate as they climbed higher, but it felt great to be out in nature in such a beautiful place. The winter rains resulted in a larger number of colorful wildflowers contrasting their bright colors against the rocky desert landscape.

After stopping to take in the views in all directions from the top of the trail, they took some photos to preserve the moment to share with their friends later in social media posts. They hadn't seen anyone else on the trail yet and were now descending the steep terrain, careful to ensure their footing was solid on some of the switchbacks where loose sand and gravel covered the path.

About an hour and fifteen minutes after they started, they were nearing the end of the western side of the trail where it met a two-lane road that they could walk along to head back toward the lot where they parked the rental car. As they turned from the last switchback on the trail about two tenths of a mile from the road, Mark noticed something that looked out of place protruding from beneath some desert scrub vegetation. Was it a dead animal? He walked toward it pensively and was suddenly overcome with the strong odor of decaying flesh. Susan called out to him asking what it was. He told Susan to stay back while he continued to approach. He held a red bandanna over his nose and mouth to filter out the stench. When he was fifteen feet away, he could see a human foot sticking out of the brush. He carefully worked his way around to get a better view, and in doing so, he saw the rest of the body. It was definitely a human being but bloated from the heat and decompositional gases being released inside of the body. He suspected it was the body of a female due to the length of the hair, but he couldn't be completely certain from this angle. He knew better than to disturb the scene or touch the remains, and deftly backed away and pulled out his mobile phone to dial 911.

The cell coverage wasn't exceptionally strong this close to the mountain, but he was able to complete the call. He explained what they had found to the dispatcher, and they were instructed to remain near the scene but close to the road where they could keep an eye on the body but could be seen by responding deputies from the Riverside County Sheriff's Department that would be arriving shortly. As the gravity of what they discovered began to sink in, Susan needed to sit down on a boulder and collect herself. She thought that she might get sick. Neither one of them had ever seen a dead body before and were certainly not expecting to see one this morning on vacation. As they awaited the deputies' response, their thoughts drifted to how this woman ended up here in the desert all alone. It was difficult for them to comprehend, and the images of what they found would likely be seared into their memory for the rest of their lives.

9

Sonny spent a couple of hours at the office while he was waiting for the security supervisor to arrive at work and let him view the video of Sharon's car entering and parking at the garage at LA Live. Before leaving the office, he reviewed information from the credit card company pertaining to Sharon's Visa credit card. It was last used on Monday afternoon at the restaurant in Beverly Hills for $82.78. No other charges had occurred since that time. That fact seemed to align with the information gleaned from her mobile phone provider. Her phone stopped pinging off the cell towers located within a few miles of the parking garage at approximately 9:45 p.m. It was possible that she was still nearby and had just turned off her phone. Or perhaps someone turned it off for her and took her away by other means. He was hoping to learn more when he saw the parking garage video.

Sonny was back at the garage and inside the security office making small talk with the camera operator when the supervisor stepped inside. "Are you the private investigator that wants to review some video involving the red Mercedes?"

"Yes, I was here early this morning but was told that you needed to approve the request," Sonny explained as he handed the man a business card. After providing his PI license and driver's license to be copied for the file, Sonny was taken to a small office nearby where the supervisor queued up the video from the previous Monday evening for camera 24, the one with a clear view of the entry and parking stall where Sharon Summerlin's car was parked. The video was paused at 6 p.m., as the supervisor was unsure when the car entered the garage. He advanced the frames at a moderate speed until Sonny told him to stop and back up a few seconds. Sonny saw the red Mercedes appear in the distance at the entry point. The time on the paused screen read 21:21:43 in military time, or 9:21 p.m. Sonny noted the time and asked him to proceed slowly. The red Mercedes pulled into the garage and passed by three rows before turning left and pulling straight into the fifth stall. The front of the car was facing toward the camera but approximately 90' away. The windows were darkly tinted, and he could not see who was driving or how many people were inside the car.

The headlights turned off and the car was still for several minutes. What was she doing? Was she waiting for someone? Then at 21:24:17, the driver's door opened, and Sharon Summerlin stepped out. She closed the door and appeared to press the button on the key fob causing the headlights to flash one time as she walked toward the exit leading up to the street. She was alone and there didn't appear to be any other vehicles parked close to her that she was moving toward, as if to meet someone else. He could see that she was wearing a summer outfit and carrying a small purse in her left hand as she entered the elevator leading up to the street. There was no camera in the elevator, but the street level lobby camera showed her walking out onto the sidewalk and turning north at 21:26:54. Five minutes after she entered the garage, she was gone.

Sonny watched the video feeds several more times before requesting that the supervisor protect them, so they did not get discarded after the normal 30-day retention period. The supervisor marked the videos and said they would now be held for 90-days in a separate folder pending any further request from the police or an order from a court. Sonny thanked him for his help and retrieved his car to leave the garage.

As Sonny pulled out into traffic, he was trying to determine where Sharon Summerlin was headed. He drove slowly north and looked at the businesses on both sides of the street to see what might make sense. There were restaurants and other street businesses nearby, but nothing that really stood out to him. It didn't seem that she would stop at a restaurant after having had a late lunch, but he couldn't rule it out. Sonny wondered if she had met someone at the Marriott hotel. He was mulling over the possibilities when his phone began to vibrate in his pocket. His mind immediately thought of Veronica Jones, as he left her a voicemail earlier in the day seeking to meet and follow-up further with her. Sonny glanced over at the center screen and saw it was Tim Patrick.

"Tim, what's going on?" Sonny answered. "Sonny, where are you?" Tim asked. "Just finished up at LA Live reviewing the video of Sharon Summerlin at the parking garage," Sonny shot back.

"We got a call from Riverside Sheriffs a little while ago. They have a white female body found by some hikers this morning near Palm Springs and were checking to see if it might be ours. Since we didn't have anything recent that fit, I immediately thought of your case. The body was naked but had been exposed to the elements for a couple of days at least," Tim explained.

Sonny paused before asking, "Does the victim have any tattoos?"

Patrick replied, "A starfish above the left ankle. Does it match up?"

Sonny's heart sank. That was the only tattoo that Jim Summerlin told him that Sharon had. A small starfish above the left ankle. "I think it's her," Sonny said slowly. While there would have to be a positive ID, things did not look good.

"I'm going to head out there. I will call her husband on the way and see if I can get him to come to the coroner's office to ID the body. Can you call someone at Riverside and pave the way for me to get some cooperation?" Sonny asked his friend.

"I am happy to make a call for you. I will text you the location and name of the officer handling the investigation and scene, while you get going," Patrick offered.

"Thanks Tim. I owe you one," Sonny said.

"Don't mention it. Let me know what you learn from the Sheriffs and what we might be able to do to assist," Patrick replied before hanging up.

Sonny headed to the 10 Freeway to go east toward Palm Springs. It would take about an hour and forty-five minutes to get there this time of day. Once he hit the freeway, he called Jim Summerlin's assistant and asked to speak to Jim. There was no good way to do this, and Sonny decided to be as direct as possible.

"Sonny, what did you see on the video?" Summerlin asked when he picked-up the call.

"Jim, I'm afraid I have some bad news. Some hikers found a body near Palm Springs this morning and I think it may be Sharon. I am on my way there now to meet with Riverside County Sheriff's investigators."

Stunned silence. Finally, Jim Summerlin spoke in a soft voice, "It doesn't make any sense. Why would she be out in the desert? Who would ever want to hurt her? Maybe it isn't Sharon. Why would they think it was her?"

"The victim has a small starfish tattoo above the left ankle," Sonny responded.

Jim was silent for about 30-seconds when Sonny asked if he could meet him at the Riverside County Coroner's office in Perris, California in a few hours to try to identify the body. Jim said he could leave in a couple of hours but would try to fly out on a helicopter and land nearby. He would text Sonny with his ETA while on the way. Sonny told him he would be waiting when he arrived, and they disconnected the call.

Jim Summerlin was in shock, Sonny thought. He just didn't know it yet. It would take some time for him to grasp what had happened, and the trip to the ME to ID the body would be one of the hardest things he would ever have to do. Sonny vowed to do everything in his power to find out what happened to Sharon Summerlin, and who was responsible for her death. They will not escape justice, he thought to himself. Not if he had anything to say about it.

10

As he came down out of a cut through some rock where the 10 Freeway levels out about 30-minutes from the Palm Springs area, Sonny's cell service picked back up and he called Steve Kurtz, his digital forensic computer expert. He wanted to follow-up on what the examination of Sharon's laptop produced. Steve answered on the first ring and after exchanging some pleasantries, began to cover all the diagnostics that he completed thus far. He outlined the keyword searches he conducted over the course of the last 24-hours. Steve was very thorough and learned his craft when employed as a computer analyst for the CIA some years ago. He was now semi-retired, working as an independent contractor for a few trusted friends.

Steve explained that there was only one Gmail account that Sharon was using on her laptop, just as her husband had said. There was nothing striking about her web queries or anything helpful that emanated from the keyword searches. While he had some additional things he wanted to try, to this point, the examination had not uncovered anything that would be very helpful. Sonny advised that the case may be taking on a much more ominous tone, as it may have moved from a missing person to a homicide investigation. Steve assured him that he would continue to grind and told Sonny to pass on anything new that he learned that might help narrow the search. Sonny provided Steve with the information on where Sharon's car was found in case that might yield something of value.

After ending the call, Sonny exited the highway and dropped south onto a two-lane road north of Palm Springs. It was 104 degrees with no clouds to be found anywhere. The mountains all around him were imposing, as they reached toward the sky. This area was quite beautiful, he thought to himself as he drove on. There was an aerial tram nearby that would take you from the desert floor up to the top of the mountain where you might find snow, even when it was this hot down in the desert. After he rounded a sharp curve to the right, he saw the flashing lights and vehicles pulled off in the distance near the base of the mountain. He identified himself to the perimeter officer and was permitted to park and walk approximately a quarter of a mile to the scene.

Detective Brian Stevens walked over and introduced himself to Sonny. "Tim Patrick from LAPD Robbery Homicide called ahead and explained that you are a former NYPD homicide detective working as a PI and might know who our victim is."

"I'm not sure, but it seems to fit with a missing person case I have been working in LA," Sonny answered. "What do you have?"

"White, female approximately 30-40 years of age. Two gunshot wounds to the back of the head at close range. Both rounds exited the front of her face. The body has been removed to the ME's office. We don't have a time of death yet but based upon the condition of the body, I'd say she has been here for 2 or 3 days. The weather has been warmer than normal for May, and that certainly will affect decomposition," Detective Stevens replied.

Sonny asked if it appeared that she was killed where the body was found. The detective felt certain that was the case. He described the exit wounds in greater detail and the working theory that the victim was standing when she was struck by the first round and was falling forward when the second round impacted her. Because of the angle of the second shot, the crime scene techs were able to recover the second slug from the ground in good condition. The detective then walked Sonny closer to the scene and pointed out the exact location where the body was found and the position it was in.

"We have some tire impressions we will cast back by the point where the trail is close to the road, but we're not sure if they are connected to the case. We also recovered the brass near the body. Looks like a 9mm," Stevens posited.

Sonny looked around but it was clear there were no homes anywhere near where the body was discovered. He asked about any traffic cameras on the 10 Freeway near the closest exit, but the detective said they did not exist in this area. "Once we have a better idea on time of death, we will put a press release out asking anyone that may have driven by on the 10 or local roads at the approximate time, and observed any stopped vehicles or anything suspicious, to contact us," Stevens said.

They walked back in the direction of Sonny's car and Stevens said he planned to meet Sonny and Jim Summerlin at the Coroner's office in an hour. Sonny proceeded to the landing zone identified by Jim Summerlin's pilot. It was located on an athletic field adjacent to a local high school but much closer to the coroner's office, about 45-minutes from the crime scene. As he awaited the arrival of the helicopter, Sonny couldn't help but flash back to some of the times in his past when he had to deliver a death message to a parent or spouse. Those encounters were extremely difficult and stayed with him for a long time afterward. It was by far the worst part of being a cop.

After the Bell 429 GlobalRanger helicopter landed, Sonny waited for the pilot to begin to shut down the engines so he wouldn't have to deal with as much rotor wash. The pilots would be standing by for what might be a few hours or so depending upon what transpired with the ID. He crouched down and walked toward the passenger door in full view of both pilots. He opened the door and a visibly shaken Jim Summerlin stepped out. Their eyes met and Sonny patted him on the shoulder as he ushered him toward his car for the 10-minute drive to meet Detective Stevens and the Coroner. On the ride over, Sonny explained what to expect and that the investigators would want to interview him further if it was Sharon. Jim acknowledged as much and braced himself for what was to come.

A short time later, they arrived at the coroner's office in Perris, CA. Sonny led Jim inside where Detective Stevens and the Deputy Coroner were waiting for them. After brief introductions, they walked down a sterile hallway into a refrigerated room with large silver drawers lining the walls. The Deputy walked to drawer #12 and opened it, slowly sliding the tray out and exposing the body laying lifeless on top of it. Sonny watched Jim's face to gauge his reaction as the drawer slid out. It appeared as if Jim's knees would give out and he would not be able to stay upright, as he realized in that instant that his wife of seven years was gone. Sonny saw his world begin to crumble around him. Even with the significant damage to her face, it was obvious to Jim Summerlin that this was his wife, Sharon. His eyes glanced down toward her feet, and he saw the starfish tattoo that he had seen so many times before when she was a vibrant woman, full of life.

"It's her. This is my wife, Sharon," Jim confirmed in a stilted, almost inaudible voice.

"Thank you, Mr. Summerlin," Detective Stevens replied. "We are very sorry for your loss. We will step outside so that you can have a moment alone," he continued before accompanying the Deputy Coroner outside into the hallway.

Sonny stood back a few steps and silently watched in case Jim needed him or wanted to ask any questions. He observed as Jim Summerlin reached down and took Sharon's left hand in his and whispered how sorry he was that he wasn't there to prevent this from happening to her. He would love her always, and promised to see whoever was responsible brought to justice. Jim stood silently next to her for several minutes with tears streaming down his face. His life was changed forever.

11

Sonny left Jim Summerlin with the detectives. They needed to conduct a formal interview and it would take some time to complete. This was now a full-fledged homicide investigation. Sonny arranged for them to take Jim back to the helicopter after they were finished.

Since he used up a lot of juice on the drive out to the desert, Sonny needed to get a quick charge for the Tesla. The car highlighted the closest charging station on his way back to LA, located on the 215 just north of the 10 in San Bernardino. It would take him about 25-minutes to get there. It was now late afternoon, and he was beginning to feel some fatigue kicking in. The sun was sapping his energy today. The sun was different out in the desert, Sonny thought to himself while shifting the car into autopilot.

He arrived and found most of the chargers to be free, so he backed the car into one on the far end and plugged in. You always wanted to position yourself with at least one space between your vehicle and the next car charging, as this would provide the fastest charging speeds. Since the car's charge was low, it would take 45-minutes to top off and prevent the need to stop at all on the way back to LA.

Sonny got back into the car while it charged and decided to take stock of what he knew so far in this case. Sharon Summerlin was last seen alive on camera at the parking garage at LA Live around 9:30 p.m. on Monday night. Her mobile phone stopped pinging the nearby cell towers at 9:45 p.m. The coroner's preliminary estimate for time of death was pegged at around 1 a.m. early Tuesday morning. Since it took approximately one hour and forty-five minutes to drive from the garage to the location in the desert where she was murdered, that left a window from roughly 9:30 p.m. to 11:15 p.m. that was unaccounted for. It was possible that she met someone outside on the street in a vehicle that transported her somewhere else. However, Sonny thought it made more sense that she selected the parking garage for a reason. She was planning to walk a short distance to do something or meet someone, before returning to her car at some later time to retrieve it and most likely go home. The question was, where was she walking to? Wherever she went was most likely close by. There was less than two hours from the time she walked out of the garage until she would have to have been in a car on the way to the desert. He called Francine and left her a message requesting her to put together a detailed report of all commercial and residential locations within a fifteen-minute walk of the garage. He asked her to break them down by category and to map them as well.

After grabbing some water and a sandwich at the adjacent shopping center, Sonny was back inside his car. The screen showed that he had eighteen minutes left on the charger. He grabbed his laptop computer from a bag in the trunk and settled back into the driver's seat. A palm tree was providing just enough shade for him to be able to see the screen at a comfortable angle. He decided to try something. Steve Kurtz did not find any indication of anything other than a lone Gmail account that Sharon used on her laptop. Sonny knew how thorough Steve was and didn't doubt the accuracy of that claim. However, while knowing it was a long shot, he began to try the same email address on various other email platforms using the same password, just in case. He tried Spectrum, Verizon, and AT&T first, but was not able to sign in using Sharon's Gmail credentials. He then typed Yahoo.com into the search bar and clicked on the mail icon in the top right corner. It opened a page where he could attempt to sign into email. Sonny carefully typed the email address and entered Sharon's Gmail password. He felt a surge of adrenaline as the Yahoo account populated and opened an inbox. However, the inbox was empty. He didn't see anything but a clean void where he would have expected to see a queue of messages. Sonny began to click onto the different file names on the left when he saw it. The Draft folder had a (1) next to it. He quickly clicked on the link, opening a draft email that had not yet been sent. It was from Sharon to Veronica Jones, dated Monday, May 4 at 9:24 p.m.

Ronnie,

Thank you for taking the time to talk with me this afternoon. You helped me tremendously, just by listening. You are a good friend. I am ashamed of my actions and am ending it with Lance tonight. Thank you for helping me to see what I need to do.

Sharon

Sonny read the message again and thought about what it meant to the case. It must have been written in the parking garage before Sharon got out of her car. That meant that she used her mobile phone to access the Yahoo email account. That would explain why the account would not necessarily be found on her laptop computer. Did she intend to send it but failed to do so and it auto saved inside her draft folder? Was she concerned and wrote it for someone to find if things went wrong? She could easily delete the message later, he thought, if things went as planned and she didn't need to tell anybody about ending it with Lance. Who was Lance? It certainly appeared that Sharon Summerlin was having an affair with someone outside of her marriage and without the knowledge of her husband. It also appeared that Veronica Jones had not told him everything that she knew when they spoke over the phone. Did this affair have something to do with her murder?

Sonny unplugged his car and headed back toward the 10 freeway. He was recharged now, in more ways than one. This was a huge break, Sonny thought. It may be the kind of break that turns the tide. Sonny had the name Lance but would need more to find him and determine if he was connected to this in some way. He knew that Veronica Jones could provide additional information that might help him learn what happened to Sharon Summerlin, and where she was going on Monday night when she disappeared. Sonny would be sure to conduct the follow-up interview with Veronica in person and without advanced warning. First thing tomorrow morning.

12

It was 6:30 a.m. when Sonny parked down the street from Veronica Jones' home in Calabasas. He put the windows down and could hear the sprinkler systems watering the greenery all around him. There was a sweet smell of flowers in the air. This was a mature, tree lined street with dense foliage providing a lush bit of privacy for the homes located close together. Veronica's home was a tasteful two story with a detached garage located in the rear. Sonny arrived early because he wanted to be sure to catch her before she left the house. He felt much better this morning following a strenuous workout last night after getting back home. He did a circuit of strength training followed by a short run to clear his mind. Sonny preferred to exercise in the morning but knew he would be leaving early and felt he could benefit from some sleep instead. All that sitting in the car needed to be offset by some serious exercise and a good meal. He went to bed early and felt refreshed this morning, still riding the momentum from yesterday's Yahoo email account discovery.

While Sonny didn't think Veronica Jones had a regular day job, he wasn't sure what she did for a living. He knew that she was single, but in case she did leave early for work, he did not want to miss the chance to speak with her as soon as possible. Sonny decided that if she didn't come out by 7:30, he would ring her doorbell. Given the circumstances, he felt that she would understand the sense of urgency.

At 6:55 a.m., Sonny saw the front door open as Veronica Jones stepped outside with what appeared to be a small dog on a leash. While he didn't want to interrupt her routine, he wasn't going to pass up the opportunity to approach her. As he closed the distance between them, he noticed that her dog was a Jack Russell terrier. As soon as the dog saw Sonny moving up the walkway toward the home, it started barking ferociously. When Veronica looked up, Sonny stopped and identified himself.

"What are you doing here at this hour?" She asked.

"I need to talk to you about Sharon. It's important. Can we go inside to speak privately?" Sonny countered.

Veronica relented and attempted to calm her small dog as she led the way back into her kitchen. They sat at a table next to the window in her breakfast nook overlooking the side yard.

Sonny began, "I'm sorry to have to tell you this but Sharon is dead. She was murdered in the desert near Palm Springs. Her body was recovered yesterday."

Veronica's mouth was agape. She didn't blink and tried to steady herself before responding. "How did she end up there? Do you know who did this to her?" Veronica stood up and went to the sink to get a glass of water before sitting back down across from Sonny. Sonny explained that he was hoping that she could help him find those responsible for her murder.

"The other day when we spoke over the phone, there was something that you were not telling me," He pointed out. "I can understand that you did not know that she may be in danger and perhaps did not want to betray her confidences by speaking out of school. However, it is now critically important that you share everything that you know that might have a bearing on her murder." He paused and studied her body language, awaiting her response. She held normal eye contact and didn't move to touch her nose or move her hands in front of her throat, any of the normal indicators of possible deception. Her breathing rate was unchanged, and her voice held steady as she began to speak.

"You're right, I held back when we spoke the other day because I didn't want to go back on my promise to her," she said. She then detailed what she knew about Sharon's affair with someone that she kept secret from her husband. "Sharon wouldn't even tell me his name. He was insistent that she could not tell anyone about him or their relationship," Veronica explained.

"Did Sharon tell you why she was not permitted to divulge his name?" Sonny asked.

Veronica replied, "I got the feeling that he had some sort of powerful position that could be compromised if the affair became public. He seemed to be controlling her. At least that is how I interpreted the situation."

Sonny then had Veronica recall the conversations that she had with Sharon about this mystery man, including the last one they had on Monday afternoon at the restaurant in Beverly Hills after they went shopping. Veronica recounted their conversation and how it appeared that Sharon was now becoming very disillusioned with him and seemed to have regrets about ever becoming involved with him in the first place. "Sharon also mentioned that what she did was not fair to Jim, that if he found out, he would be crushed," she explained.

Veronica said that she mainly just listened to her friend without passing judgement or providing any unsolicited advice. She characterized it as believing that Sharon wanted to get some things off her chest to decide what to do next. "Before she left, she told me she had some more thinking to do but thanked me for listening to her."

Sonny then asked if Veronica knew anyone named Lance that could be connected to Sharon. "You mean that's his name, Lance? That is the guy she was seeing?" Sharon asked.

"I'm not sure but that could be his name. I don't know his last name yet, but he is involved in this somehow, and I need to identify him," Sonny replied. "Think hard. Did she ever mention anyone named Lance or do you recall any acquaintance by that name that she could have connected with? Anyone at the club?"

Veronica looked up and her forehead wrinkled as she seemed to be searching her mind for any possible connection that might help. "I'm sorry. I can't think of anyone named Lance that I know, let alone someone connected to Sharon."

Before he left, Sonny asked her to call him at any time if she remembered more about her conversations with Sharon that involved the affair. He also asked her to go back through her text messages with Sharon and to let him know if it jogged her memory further for anything that might help.

"Do you think that Lance, or the person she was involved with, killed her?" Veronica asked in a low voice.

"I'm not sure if the affair is connected to her murder at this point. There are just too many unknowns right now," Sonny answered. "But," he continued, "I do intend to find out."

Sonny let himself out and walked back to his car. He dialed the office and left a message for Francine. He wanted her to use their systems to try to put a list together of men in the Los Angeles area with the first name of Lance that held powerful positions in the motion picture, music, entertainment, or government fields. Any position where the person held a prominent role that could be affected by negative publicity or marital indiscretions. Francine would receive the message as soon as she got into the office in an hour or so. Sonny decided to grab breakfast at a diner on the PCH on his way to the office.

13

Lance (Monday, four days earlier)

Lance Frederick stared out the window of his office in City Hall and wondered exactly how it had reached this point. He had clawed his way into a position of power and influence as the Chief of Staff to the Mayor of the City of Los Angeles. He knew how to play the game and turn on the charm to adapt to any situation, to achieve whatever manipulative result he desired. Only this time, the situation may have gotten away from him and left him with few viable options.

He was not born into privilege, but always seemed destined to get there. Lance would stop at nothing to get what he wanted. As a child, he learned how to curry favor with his teachers to gain some sort of advantage over his classmates. Life was a zero-sum game to him, even if he pretended to be a man of compromise, always trying to improve the situation of others. In truth, he was only concerned with how he could benefit from any relationship that he engaged in.

Before opening his own political consulting firm, Lance ingratiated himself to the current mayor while working for a prominent LA lobbying firm. He was very comfortable navigating the political currents that swirled around city and county government here in the City of Angels. He could spot an up-and-coming talent and elbowed his way past his colleagues to handle the political interests of Wilfredo Sosa before anyone saw

Sosa's true potential in wooing the local electorate. In the beginning, Sosa was an outsider launching a campaign for City Council while representing a largely Hispanic district. Early on, Lance saw something in the handsome, soft spoken, budding politician. Something that he felt he could harness and ride to a position where he would run the show and benefit from controlling access to power.

After winning a seat on City Council, several external events conspired to put Sosa in a position to leverage his popularity and newfound influence in a much larger way. The growing Latino population in the city was beginning to realize that they could be a formidable force if they exerted themselves in a coordinated fashion. The killing of an unarmed Hispanic male by SWAT team personnel outside of a local Mexican restaurant vaulted Sosa into the spotlight. The timing could not have been more fortuitous, as Sosa had found his voice and confidence over the last several years in representing the people of his district. Sosa had staked out a position of police accountability and was a vocal critic of the LAPD's tactics. At this moment, Lance helped craft the message that Sosa would use to make his case that a change was needed at City Hall, and it was time for a Latino mayor. A mayor that could truly identify with the plight of those that were underrepresented in the halls of power. That fall, Sosa won a close election that assured Lance Frederick of attaining the goal that he had worked for over the course of many years. He had finally arrived.

Lance was named as the Mayor's Chief of Staff and assisted Sosa in filling the important roles that would make up his cabinet at City Hall. At every step along the way, Lance was able to exert his influence in a way that would ultimately benefit him in the long run.

He met Sharon Summerlin at a fundraiser one night at the Beverly Hills Hotel. Lance spotted her from across the room and circled her like the shark that he was, awaiting the perfect time to sink his sharp teeth into her. She was very attractive and athletic looking, traits that he found pleasing. Lance wasn't looking for some sort of long-term relationship but wanted to add her to his regular stable of eye-catching female companions. She was married to a prominent entertainment industry leader, but that just made him want her more. Lance liked to take things that didn't belong to him, and this would be no different. He sensed some vulnerability in her, and turned on the charm to lure her in.

Because she was married, and due to his prominent position in the city, Lance insisted that their relationship be completely confidential. He made her swear not to divulge it to even her best friend. They did not meet at his home in Pacific Palisades or at her home in Malibu, but instead kept everything strictly on the down low. While she was not the only person he saw, he was sure that she was only stepping outside of her marriage with him.

Recently, however, things began to sour. Perhaps he was beginning to drop the elaborate façade a little too much around her and she awakened to discover the type of person he really was. Lance began to lose his patience with her, and really lost it when he caught her going through the text messages on his confidential phone. In fact, it was that action on her part that forced him to this point. She knew better than to do what she did, and now he couldn't be sure that she had not connected the dots to his friends in Las Vegas, putting everything and everyone at risk.

Faced with a critical decision, Lance only saw two options available to him. Option one involved going to the police and exposing both a contract bid rigging scheme, and the mob connections attempting to influence a commercial real estate development project that the mayor's office could push in the direction sought by organized crime. That, however, would most surely result in a predictable outcome. Lance would be indicted by the local U.S. Attorney for public corruption violations and embezzlement of funds pertaining to the substantial kickbacks that he received from the mob for steering them contracts and obtaining the zoning approvals that they needed. The current federal prosecutor had grand political ambitions and was using his "public corruption" platform to go after every high-ranking politician that showed even a momentary lapse in judgement. He would view Lance's actions as far more than a small transgression, and no doubt attempt to ensnare the mayor as well. No, he did not relish the idea of spending a decade or two in federal prison while also being stripped of all the money he had worked so hard to secure along the way. His reputation would be ruined, and he would be left penniless with no way to support the lifestyle that he felt he deserved.

Option two involved sticking to the agreement he had forged with the mobsters in Las Vegas. Lance would immediately inform them that he caught her reading incriminating messages between them that detailed portions of their criminal conspiracy. While they would not be happy with him for allowing that to happen, they would ensure the loose end was tied up. Unfortunately for Sharon Summerlin, option two would not end well for her.

It didn't take Lance long to rationalize his way to choosing option two. After all, she made the decision to become involved with him in the first place. She was the one that violated his trust by poking around where she shouldn't have, and if he couldn't trust her not to do that, could he really trust her not to divulge the nature of their relationship? Was he really willing to take that chance and risk everything because of this woman?

After compartmentalizing his decision, Lance made the call to Las Vegas. His call irretrievably set in motion a series of events that would alter the lives of many people. Some of those lives would be altered in the immediate future in a permanent way.

14

When Sonny arrived at the office, Francine was already hard at work. "Looks like you have been here for awhile," he remarked as he closed the door behind him.

"Yes, I came in early today. I checked my messages remotely last night and knew that you needed the information on the businesses within a 15-minute walk of the parking garage. When I got here today, I played your second message about finding people that fit the profile with the first name of Lance in the Los Angeles County area. I decided to start with that, and I put the information on your desk. I'm currently working on the business report," Francine stated proudly.

"Once again, you are the best. I will be sure to add that to the list to offset the next time you need to take a long weekend," he replied.

"Funny you should mention that. I was thinking about camping with friends next weekend in Joshua Tree. I might look to cash that in!"

"You got it. Let me know what you come up with regarding the businesses. I'm going to start working on Lance," he said as he walked into his office.

Sonny sat down behind the desk and began to read the information that Francine prepared for him. Apparently, there were approximately 104,000 people with the first name of Lance in the US, with 3,170 of them residing in Los Angeles County. That was certainly more than he thought there would be. After eliminating anyone under the age of 25 and separating out those with known jobs that placed them in a position of power with a public profile, he was left with a list of 35 individuals. As he pondered the remaining names and occupations, 3 of them seemed to stick out to him.

The first was a front office executive with the Dodgers named Lance Johnson. Johnson was a former player that was well liked and recognized for his time in the big leagues. He developed himself as a scout and worked his way up the organization into his current role. He was married with two children and did not have the reputation as a risk taker among his peers. There were no salacious reports of extracurricular activities or anything out of the ordinary. That didn't mean that he was incapable of having a girlfriend on the side, and his travel schedule might afford him the chance to meet on the road. He would certainly have a lot to lose if discovered, both personally and professionally.

The second individual that made the short list was a recording executive and producer named Lance Washington. He was a former music performer that started his own record label and built a stable of talent before selling his interests just prior to the music industry going digital. He then parlayed that into a senior role with Live Nation in talent acquisition. He knew the right people in the music and entertainment field in LA and could be counted on to deliver top names for a project. He was married to a reality TV star who had a huge following on social media. It was rumored that she was now making more money than he was. He also would have some risk if he was discovered to be dating someone on the side. The fact that he moved in some of the same circles as Jim Summerlin also presented a potential opportunity to have met Sharon at some point along the way.

The third person was Lance Frederick, the Chief of Staff to the current Mayor of Los Angeles, Wilfredo Sosa. Frederick was known as a mover and shaker in the political world, mainly in Southern California. He was wired in at all levels of government and was the gatekeeper to the mayor. Nothing happened without it going through him. Mayor Sosa had crafted an image as a crusader against corruption, especially heavy-handed actions by the LAPD. He also painted himself as a staunch family man with a wife and five children. Frederick was not married but would risk negative publicity for the mayor if he were exposed as cheating with the wife of a prominent studio executive. There would certainly be repercussions given his high-profile role and the interest the story would generate with the local media.

As Sonny sat back and considered the three men, he felt that he would most likely need to do a deeper dive on each of them, including an interview to gauge their reactions in person. That might be more difficult than it seemed, as all three were insulated somewhat from the outside world due to their status. He decided that he would start with Lance Frederick, as he was probably a little more accessible than the other two. And he heard on the radio that the mayor was scheduled to address his plan to curb homelessness at noon today in front of the Los Angeles County Museum of Art. There was a decent chance that his Chief of Staff would attend the event. Sonny decided that he would be there as well.

Sonny looked at his watch. If he hustled, he would have enough time to change clothes and do a 45-minute power walk in Runyon Canyon. He changed into workout gear and told Francine he was going to hike the canyon and would be back in time to get cleaned up and head to the museum. He liked to hike all over Los Angeles because it got him away from people and cars and more in touch with nature. Also, he often found that he could think more clearly during these hikes.

He worked his way over to Franklin and up to the park entrance. There weren't as many people here later in the morning because it started to get warm by then. Still, Sonny passed plenty of people walking their dogs and the occasional person running all the way to the top. He had great respect for those that could do their running workout on a hiking trail and not collapse. Sonny considered himself very fit but would not be able to do that. He could hike fast, but running was something all together different on these steep inclines.

Sonny worked up a sweat climbing methodically in the morning sun. He stopped when he reached the top of the trail to take in the view of Hollywood below and downtown in the distance. This view never disappointed, he thought. The trail was popular because it was so close to civilization but took you to another world in a matter of minutes. Off to his left he could see the Hollywood sign and the Griffith Observatory. As he looked over the City of Angels, his thoughts returned to Sharon Summerlin. He needed to push forward and learn the truth about her murder. Someone out there knows what happened, he thought. He was determined to find those responsible and expose them for what they really were, cold blooded killers.

15

Sonny arrived at the Museum of Art twenty minutes before the mayor was scheduled to speak. There was a podium set up on the plaza directly in front of the Urban Light art display, a compilation of 202 solar powered cast iron streetlamps arranged in neat rows. The theme of the mayor's remarks apparently would use the Urban Light exhibit to highlight his new Urban Light to End Homelessness initiative. There were several camera crews and both print and electronic media gathered on folding chairs arranged facing the podium. It also appeared that a few of the local homeless population intended to take in the press conference as well.

Sonny stood across Wilshire where he could scan the crowd without drawing any attention to himself. He would cross the street just before the event began. The usual routine involved setting the time for noon to capture the lunchtime news broadcasts and anyone that might be outside getting something to eat from a local food truck. Usually, the mayor would not begin speaking until about eight or ten minutes after the appointed start time. Sonny saw the mayor's press secretary speaking with local reporters near the podium. He also saw several of the mayor's security detail taking positions off to both sides to be out of the shot but close enough to respond to any threat. He didn't see the chief of staff, but assumed he was probably inside the museum with the mayor preparing him for the event.

At 12:03 p.m., Sonny began to make his way across Wilshire to take a position near the rear of the crowd. A couple of minutes after he was in place, two of the mayor's security detail could be seen escorting the mayor from inside the museum to the podium on the plaza. And right behind the mayor was Lance Frederick, giving him some last second advice by whispering into his ear. Once the mayor was introduced and began to outline his new initiative, Lance faded off to the side and consulted something in a binder he carried with him. Sonny was wearing sunglasses, so he could easily keep his focus on Lance the entire time without drawing any attention. He studied Lance just to get a feel for him. Lance fidgeted around and looked at his phone while also listening to the mayor's remarks. After about fifteen minutes, the prepared portion of the event was complete, and the press secretary opened it up for a few questions from the assembled media. As this was happening, Lance continued to work his phone, no doubt sending important messages to his underlings.

After the press secretary concluded the formal Q&A, the mayor was ushered off to the side for a couple of stand-up camera interviews for live shots on local broadcasts. As this was transpiring, Sonny saw Lance drift back behind a few rows of the streetlamps to take a phone call. Sonny took this opportunity to work his way through the media as they packed up their equipment and prepared to move on to their next assignment. The security detail was focused on the mayor and those near him and paid no attention to Sonny. He took an angle that would permit him to keep Lance in his field of view but approach in a way that he would not expose himself until he was right next to Lance. When he observed that Lance was finishing the call and beginning to shift back towards the plaza, Sonny moved in.

"Mr. Frederick, my name is Sonny Romano, do you have a moment?" Sonny was directly in his path and the streetlamps on either side provided effective barriers, preventing Lance from avoiding the conversation.

"I am pretty busy right now," Lance replied in an annoyed and condescending tone. "I need to get back to the mayor."

"This will only take a second," Sonny countered. "I want to ask you about a friend of yours, Sharon Summerlin." Sonny watched Lance closely and saw a slight tell as his face tensed up and he swallowed hard before responding.

"Who? I'm afraid I don't know anyone by that name," Lance retorted, trying to play it off in a casual manner, but looking very agitated. "You must have me confused with someone else."

"No, Sharon referred specifically to you," Sonny lied.

"What is this about? What media outlet are you with?" Lance shot back angrily.

"I'm not a member of the media. I'm a private investigator. When was the last time that you communicated with Sharon?"

"I told you; I don't know who she is. I've never met her, and you have obviously made a mistake. Now if you will excuse me, I have work to do."

"Where were you last Monday evening?" Sonny asked.

"I was with the mayor at a fundraiser in Santa Monica from 9 p.m. until after midnight, if you must know. Now get out of my way," Lance was clearly losing his composure.

Sonny stepped aside and Lance quickly walked away without looking back. Jackpot, Sonny thought to himself as he watched Lance Frederick move back toward the mayor. His instincts told him this guy was involved. He definitely knew Sharon, and if that were true, he knew her as more than a casual acquaintance. It didn't mean that he had anything to do with her murder, but his denials needed to be thoroughly investigated and run to ground. Sonny had some legwork to do and couldn't wait to get started.

16

As soon as he got back in the car, Sonny called Francine and asked her to pull up the mayor's fundraising event schedule from his re-election website. She confirmed that there was an event listed the previous Monday evening at the JW Marriott in Santa Monica. Sonny thanked her and said that he was going to swing out to Santa Monica before heading back into the office. He also asked her to pull everything she could on Lance Frederick from Thomson Reuters so that he could review it as soon as he returned to the office. She told him she would get right on it and advised him that she finished the business listing and mapping that he requested using the parking garage as the center point.

"Fantastic, I will look at that as well," he replied. "I should be back around 3 p.m."

"See you then," Francine said.

Sonny really wanted to find a connection between Sharon and Lance. He was determined to explore every possible lead that he could to do so. First, however, he wanted to see if he could verify the alibi that Lance put forward regarding the fundraiser last Monday night. He suspected that it was true, as it wouldn't be too difficult to disprove it if he was lying. If it was true, it meant that Lance could not have been downtown if he was out in Santa Monica between 9 p.m. and midnight. Sharon's phone stopped pinging the towers at 9:45 p.m., and she would have had to have been moving toward the desert by about 11:15 p.m. This would be a strong alibi for Lance against having physically been involved in Sharon's disappearance after leaving the parking garage. A very convenient one that Lance seemed to have ready to go when Sonny posed the question. It didn't mean that Lance wasn't involved somehow, it just meant that he wasn't physically involved. First things first, he thought to himself as he worked his way out to the JW Marriott.

When he arrived at the JW Marriott, Sonny went to the front desk and tracked down the hotel's events manager. She would be in the best position to provide the information that he needed regarding the fundraiser that occurred on Monday night. A few minutes after he made the request, the events manager appeared in the lobby to meet him.

"I'm Diane Folsom. What can I do for you?"

Sonny introduced himself and handed her a business card. "I am here to learn about the fundraiser held this past Monday night for the mayor. Are you familiar with it?"

"Yes," Diane replied. "Since it involved the mayor and VIP's, I coordinated the event myself and worked it along with a few of my staff."

Sonny felt fortunate that she was personally involved in the event and asked her some questions as they walked to the ballroom that was used for the fundraiser.

"Tell me a little about the event. When did it start and end and who was your point of contact?"

Diane responded, "The event was supposed to run from 9 p.m. until midnight. We were set and ready to go at 8 p.m., and the mayor's campaign manager was my POC. He was here at 8 p.m., and we made some minor adjustments to how the room was set, and then people started arriving just before 9 p.m. There were some heavyweight donors and important people that attended."

"What time did it end?" Sonny asked.

"They didn't leave until 12:45 a.m. We had to wait around for all of them to leave before we could have staff flip the room for a breakfast meeting early Tuesday morning," she responded.

Sonny asked if she knew who Lance Frederick was and showed her a photo. She said that she remembered Lance because he arrived with the mayor at about 9 p.m., and was rude to her when she asked him if they would be leaving soon at 12:30 a.m.

"He told me they would leave when they were finished, and we would just have to wait," she explained. "I didn't care for his attitude. He acted like he was so important, and everyone should just bow down to him. I had staff waiting around in the back hallway that were tired and needed to tear everything down and set up the Tuesday breakfast and be back in by 7 a.m." She went on to explain that the mayor was cordial and had stayed after to speak with the campaign manager and Lance Frederick before leaving with his security detail.

Sonny thanked her for her assistance and made his way back through the lobby and out to the street. He assumed the alibi would stick but felt fortunate that he was able to confirm it conclusively, especially as it related to the times Lance arrived and left the hotel. It was clear that Lance could not have been physically involved in Sharon's disappearance, and Sonny wondered if Lance purposely used this event to provide himself an alibi that could be publicly confirmed. Time will tell, he thought to himself.

Twenty-five minutes later, he was back at his office in Hollywood. Francine was nice enough to grab him a couple of fish tacos from a taco truck that he liked, before the guy left for the day. As he devoured the tacos at his desk, he began to review the business listings within a 15-minute walk of the parking garage. The list was broken down by business type, and he laid that document on the left side of his desk with the map on the right side. The map provided an aerial view of the business locations with a circle drawn to indicate a .75-mile circumference around the parking garage. That was about as far as someone could walk in fifteen minutes at 3 miles per hour.

Sonny reviewed this information closely but came back to his initial impression that Sharon may have walked to a nearby hotel or eatery to meet someone else. He decided that he would need to do a canvass of the most likely locations to see if someone would remember her from Monday night. Because of the location at LA Live, most of the restaurants stayed open until 10 p.m., due to the normal foot traffic in the area. The hotels were open later, as bars operated until 2 a.m. He would hit the most likely locations on Monday night at around the same time that she would have been there a week prior. He highlighted the businesses he would start with in yellow, before putting the map and list into his backpack along with 12 photos of Sharon.

Next, he slid open the file folder containing the detailed background information on Lance Frederick. He took out a notepad to capture any details that he felt needed additional review or follow-up utilizing other means. Sonny made note of Lance's home address in Pacific Palisades. He would have to take a ride by to see it for himself. Fairly pricey neighborhood for a public servant, he thought as he continued to read further. There was information listed on all aspects of his life from a public records standpoint. He had no liens, bankruptcies, or criminal arrests. Only a few traffic citations from 20 years ago, and no civil judgements against him.

As he reviewed the section on employment, Sonny saw something that he had not considered. He knew that Lance worked for a large lobbying firm for several years. However, the report also displayed the name LJF Consulting, LLC, opened in California in 2008. Sonny did not know that Lance had his own consulting firm, and it appeared that the firm was still in an active status. Sonny refreshed his computer and went to the California Department of State website. Sonny knew that if you operated a business in California, you had to list an actual address for service of process, not just a P.O. Box somewhere. You could designate a resident agent for the business, but still needed an actual address in California with the Department of State. This address was discoverable by using the website if you knew how to search for it. Sonny wanted to verify that the firm was in good standing and that the Pacific Palisades address was listed with the Department of State. When he queried the website, he was very surprised to learn that the registered address for the business was different than the one listed for Lance's personal residence. It was a downtown address. He immediately went to Google maps and typed in the address listed. Sonny was elated to see that the address was located inside of the .75-mile circle surrounding the parking garage. In fact, it was a condo building on his list, about a 10-minute walk north of the parking garage. This condo address was not located anywhere else in the report as being associated with Lance Frederick. It was possible that Lance used it as his business location and linked it to LJF Consulting, LLC for tax purposes. A short walk from City Hall, it would provide a perfect crash pad if Lance worked late and didn't want to drive all the way home, especially if he had to be in early the next morning.

Sonny nearly jumped out of his chair. He grabbed his backpack and flung his office door open, startling Francine. "What is up with you?"

"I may have found something that could link Lance to Sharon. A condo downtown near the parking garage. It is within the .75-mile radius, and I didn't know about it until right now. I am heading over there to see what I can find out," Sonny proclaimed in a determined manner.

"Okay, that sounds promising. I will have my cell with me in case you need anything after I leave for the day," Francine replied.

Sonny was already moving toward the stairwell. He did not want to slow his forward momentum. His gut told him that this was significant, and he did not want to waste any time. He had Lance firmly in his sights.

17

Sonny thought about Jim Summerlin on his way downtown. He wanted to update Jim on the status of the case but decided to wait until he knew more about Lance and the potential address that he just discovered. He felt a little awkward when he considered that he may need to divulge the fact that it appeared that Sharon was seeing someone on the side. Jim has been through a lot in the past four days and was now planning Sharon's funeral services. He was also trying to comprehend how this could have happened and why. Sonny knew that he could help him by learning the truth. He was committed to doing so.

As Sonny made his way down South Figueroa Street, he decided to park in the underground garage and walk to the condo building, as Sharon may have done. He parked in the same section of the garage and set the stopwatch on his watch before beginning to walk toward the exit, taking the elevator up a floor and out onto the street. Sonny walked in a deliberate manner but did not hurry and crossed only at intersections using the most direct path to get to the condo. Traffic in the area was picking up as people tried to flee downtown on Friday afternoon to get a jump on the weekend. Angelenos were used to ridiculous traffic, but on Fridays, it seemed like everyone was looking to shave even a few minutes off the normal slog. As he passed several businesses with cameras mounted above their entryways, he wondered if there might be some video confirming that Sharon took this same route last Monday night. It would have been dark then, unlike the late afternoon daylight conditions that he was experiencing.

As Sonny waited for the walk signal at the last intersection that he needed to cross, he took in the view of the condo across the street. It was red brick and about 12 stories tall. There were balconies overlooking the city below. There appeared to be a street entrance directly ahead, as well as a parking entrance on the east side that was on a lower plane since the building was positioned on the crest of a hill. As the light changed, he crossed the intersection in front of a $200,000 Bentley convertible. The guy driving looked to be in his early seventies, but the blond in the passenger seat couldn't have been older than 30. Sonny wondered what it was like to date someone four decades younger than yourself. He smiled as he stepped onto the curb before pausing under a large Jacaranda tree. Sonny stopped the timer on his watch. 9 minutes and 12 seconds. He decided to enter through the parking entrance and proceeded down the hill toward the east side of the building.

As he approached the parking entrance, Sonny stopped to watch for a few minutes to see how building access control operated. There was a card reader of some sort about four feet tall next to an arm that was in the down position blocking vehicle access. After a minute or so, a silver Lexus pulled into the lot and approached the parking entry. The woman driving lowered her window and waved something in her hand across the surface of the reader causing the arm to lift so that she could pull her car inside. The arm then went down immediately after her vehicle passed through. Sonny noticed two cameras, one mounted up high pointed toward the reader, and another at ground level shooting the vehicles from the rear, most likely to capture the rear plate. He made a note of these observations and walked around to the front of the building to enter.

As soon as he entered, Sonny saw a concierge desk along the right wall and two elevators directly in front of him. There was a sign proclaiming that "all visitors must be escorted by residents." There were a couple more cameras mounted in the lobby, one aimed at the front door and the other covering the desk and elevators. The man at the desk was putting some dry cleaning into a closet behind him when Sonny walked up. "Good afternoon. My name is Sonny Romano. I am a private investigator working on a case and would like to speak with whomever you have working security here." The man studied him for a moment and replied that he would call Manny on the radio and ask him to stop by the desk. He motioned for Sonny to have a seat on a decorative bench next to some planters with colorful red, orange, and dark blue flowers that appeared to be well cared for. Sonny took a seat and waited for Manny while thinking of how he may want to play this.

Manny arrived a short time later on the elevator and stepped out wearing tan pants and a blue blazer with the building name embroidered on the left breast pocket. He was dark-skinned and appeared to be Hispanic and was carrying a portable radio in his left hand. He looked to be in his late twenties. Sonny stood and introduced himself. "Do you have an office where we might be able to speak privately?" Sonny asked. Manny led the way through a door in the corner of the lobby and down a stairwell to a small suite of staff offices. They walked past two administrative offices before stepping into the last one on the right labeled 'security'.

Manny asked, "How can I assist you?" Sonny began by providing some information on his background before explaining that he was working a missing person case and had reason to believe the individual may have entered the condo building on Monday evening before she went missing. Sonny motioned to the array of monitors located on the wall adjacent to the desk where Manny was sitting. "Do you have access to the lobby, elevator and parking garage video from Monday night?" Sonny asked directly. As Manny studied him while formulating a reply, Sonny pointed to the Dodgers pennant on the wall. "Are you a Dodgers fan, Manny?"

Manny stopped his train of thought and glanced to his right at the pennant. "Yes, I have been all my life. I grew up in South LA and there were a bunch of Eight Trey Gangster Crips nearby. My Mom thought it was safer to be wearing blue, and she bought me some Dodger gear when I was a kid. It took off from there."

Sonny replied, "I happen to have a couple of tickets to the game Saturday night against the Giants that I can't use and would be happy to let you have them at no cost since you are a big fan." Sonny was not above using anything at his disposal to his advantage. He had a partial season ticket plan with two seats in right field near the wall for just these occasions.

"Are you serious?" Manny blurted out excitedly. "I hate the Giants. I would love to go to the ravine and see our boys put a whooping on them."

"I can make a call and have the tickets waiting for you at the Will Call window under your name, no problem at all," said Sonny assuredly. He knew he had him right where he wanted him now. "I will make the call as soon as we finish up here." Sonny then steered the conversation back to the video.

"I'm not really supposed to let people look at the video unless there is a court order or to help the police," Manny began. "But, seeing as you are a retired cop and this is a missing person case, I guess it wouldn't hurt to take a look just in case."

"Thanks Manny. I appreciate your willingness to help. I am trying to learn the truth about what might have happened to this young lady."

"Sure. Whatever you need," Manny replied.

Sonny began by having Manny explain exactly how the access control system worked. Manny outlined the fact that each resident owner is issued two fobs that are connected to their residence account and cross referenced in the computer system to the resident on file listed as the legal owner of the condo. Each fob has a unique serial number, but both are registered to the owner of record. When the fob is placed within 6-inches of the parking garage reader, it lifts the parking arm and notes the resident's last name, serial number of the fob used and the date and time the fob was used to enter the parking garage. Likewise, the elevator in the garage or in the lobby will not open unless a fob is presented at the reader at each location. In both cases, the resident's name, serial number of the fob used and date and time the elevator was accessed, is logged by the system. This prevents a non-resident from gaining unauthorized access to the residential floors within the building. There is a unique key needed to open any of the units, but access to the elevators to enter the residence floors from outside is strictly controlled. "There is no need to use a fob to call the elevator once you are inside the building on the residence floors," Manny explained.

All of this was very interesting to Sonny. He was focused on every word and determining the way he wanted to approach this. He started by asking Manny to query the system to see if any of the fobs assigned to Lance Frederick were used last Monday evening, starting at 6 p.m. Manny confirmed that Lance Frederick owned a condo on the 12th floor with a view facing west. It was a two-bedroom unit located down the hall away from the elevator landing. Manny advised that there were cameras on each floor focused only on the elevator. There were no cameras covering the hallways immediately outside of each residence for privacy purposes.

As Manny typed the search parameters into the video management system software, Sonny glanced at the monitors on the wall to see what angles would be covered in both the lobby and at the parking garage entrance. He felt that the lobby view would be clear anytime, and the parking garage might be affected more by the lighting conditions present at a given the time of the day.

"Here is what I found," Manny declared. "It looks like Mr. Frederick's fobs were used three times on Monday between 6 p.m. and midnight. The first entry shows fob #729 at 8:24 p.m. entering the parking garage. Fob #729 was then used to call the parking garage elevator at 8:28 p.m. Then, fob #730 is used to call the elevator in the lobby at 9:39 p.m."

"So, are these the only fobs that are registered to Lance Frederick?" Sonny asked.

"Yes, they are the only ones that correspond to Mr. Frederick," Manny answered.

Sonny asked Manny if he could determine if one of the fobs was used more often than the other. Manny checked and found that fob #729 was used at least twice per day, nearly every day of the week. Then he checked fob #730.

"The other fob wasn't used more than a few times a month. However, it looks like it was reported as lost by Mr. Frederick last Tuesday afternoon," said Manny. "He was issued a replacement fob the same day by maintenance, fob #917."

Sonny pondered whether it was significant that Lance reported one of his fobs as lost the day after Sharon went missing. He would come back to that.

"Let's call up the camera feeds that correspond to these three events," requested Sonny.

"I'm on it," replied Manny.

Manny pulled up video from the parking garage entry camera from 8:24 p.m. Monday evening and played it on one of the large monitors. The video showed a blue Toyota Camry with two large men inside waiting for the parking arm to lift. The driver's face was clear because the driver's window was rolled down. The passenger's face was shaded by the shadows and window glare. After the vehicle pulled forward into the garage, Manny pulled up the ground camera and paused it with the rear license plate visible. Sonny made a note of the plate number and the fact that the car was registered in Nevada.

"Can you print a photo of the driver at the gate as well as the rear view of the car for me?" Sonny asked.

"I can print whatever stills you want when we are done," Manny answered.

Sonny then requested a view of the parking garage elevator landing from 8:24 p.m. on. Manny pulled it up on the monitor. It showed the elevator doors and area around the landing with nobody nearby for the first few minutes. At 8:27 p.m., the two large men from the Toyota Camry appeared from the right side of the frame and approached the elevator.

"Pause it right there," Sonny directed. Manny complied and Sonny studied the image. The initial image was of the driver, as he entered the frame first. He looked to be about 6' 3" tall and well over 300 lbs. He had dark hair and was attired in slacks, an open collared shirt, and a sport coat. He had several rings on his left hand and reminded Sonny of some of the people he grew up around in Italian neighborhoods in New York and North Jersey. The second guy was at least 6'2" tall and at least 250 lbs., also with dark wavy hair and dressed in a similar fashion. Of note, the second guy was pulling an empty luggage cart along with him. The driver held up the fob and the elevator light above lit up signifying that the elevator had been called. This corresponded with the time stamp reported by Manny of fob #729 at 8:28 p.m.

"Where did the cart come from?" Sonny asked.

"We have two carts that are normally stored in the elevator vestibule in case owners need help bringing up groceries or luggage to their condos," Manny responded.

Sonny noted to himself that apparently these two were going to need the cart to remove something from upstairs. Sonny had a pretty good idea of what that might be.

"Let's move to the lobby camera, beginning at 8:00 p.m. just to see what was happening on Monday night," Sonny said. "Then we can focus in on the second fob at 9:39 p.m."

Manny did as directed and moved the video onto the large monitor. He went through it slightly faster than normal speed and stopped when anything was observed to occur. There were two food deliveries noted before 9:00 p.m. and some dry cleaning delivered at 9:15 p.m. to the concierge desk. Otherwise, nothing else of importance happened until 9:38 p.m. when Sharon Summerlin appeared walking into the lobby from the street wearing the same outfit Sonny observed when she parked her car at LA Live approximately 11-minutes earlier. She went directly to the elevator but appeared to say hello as she passed the desk. At 9:39 p.m., she pulled fob #730 and summoned the elevator. A short time later, she stepped inside, and the doors closed behind her.

Sonny asked Manny to switch over to the camera view of the 12th floor elevator landing beginning at 8:00 p.m. This would correspond to the time right before the two men boarded the elevator in the parking garage at 8:28 p.m. The camera provided an elevated view of the two elevator doors and immediate area nearby but did not capture the hallways in either direction. Manny scrolled through slowly for any signs of motion. At 8:29 p.m., the right elevator door opened, and the two large men stepped off with the second man pulling the empty luggage cart beside him. They went to the right and disappeared out of the camera's view. Sonny confirmed with Manny that Lance Frederick's condo, #1243, was located near the end of the hallway on the north side of the building. This was the direction the two men went.

Manny continued to scroll through the video from the 12th floor elevator landing. Nothing was noted until 8:40 p.m., when the left door opened, and Sharon Summerlin appeared. "Pause it there," Sonny directed. Manny complied. The camera froze on Sharon as she was exiting the elevator. Sonny couldn't be certain from the image, but it appeared that she had a serious look on her face. Was she planning to meet Lance and break things off? Sonny wondered that to himself. Perhaps Lance told her to meet him at the condo that evening knowing he would not be there and would have a solid alibi as to his whereabouts. Maybe Lance had another plan in store for her.

Sonny motioned to Manny to move the video forward. Sharon went to her right in the direction of Lance's condo. She disappeared from the camera's view and Sonny couldn't help but think that she also disappeared from the rest of her life.

Since there were no more registered uses of the fobs belonging to Lance that evening, Sonny directed Manny to slowly move the video forward from 8:40 p.m. on to determine if anything else occurred near the elevators on the 12th floor. If any of them left, they would not have needed to use the fob to call the elevator from the 12th floor. Of course, it was also possible to take the stairs and avoid the camera. Sonny would cross that bridge if it became necessary.

There was zero activity observed by Sonny and Manny until 11:04 p.m. Suddenly, the two large men appeared from the left side of the screen. This time, both of them had one hand on either end of the luggage cart, one was pulling while the other pushed from behind. Manny paused the image and they both studied it. "There is something on the cart," Manny blurted out. Sonny could see what appeared to be clothing or a dark colored blanket piled up on the cart approximately halfway up. It was impossible to tell what was under the blanket, but it had to be something heavier than clothing or a blanket for the two men to both be involved in moving it toward the elevator. As the video continued, Sonny studied the mass on the cart for signs of any movement but could not detect anything. Maybe she was unconscious, he thought to himself. It made sense to knock her out for the trip down to the car so as not to draw any unwanted attention. Since her murder happened in the desert, Sonny knew if she was on the cart, she was still alive at this point in time.

Manny pulled up the parking garage camera feed next. At 11:05 p.m., the camera showed the right door open, and the two men maneuvered the cart in the direction of their parked car. A few minutes later, the Toyota Camry exited the parking garage heading east.

Sonny and Manny spent the next hour wading through video to determine when Lance returned to the condo. He did not come back that night following the event with the mayor and likely went to his home in Pacific Palisades instead. An effort to distance himself from whatever happened inside his condo that night, Sonny thought. In fact, Lance did not surface until just after 2 o'clock p.m. on Tuesday afternoon. His car was seen pulling up to the garage entrance with Lance behind the wheel. He did not use a fob, but instead pushed the button to contact the desk and appeared to be animated and engaged in gesturing to the person speaking to him from inside the building.

"He didn't have his fob," Manny said. "It looks like he probably spoke to the desk person and since they knew him, they buzzed him into the garage. He got his new fob shortly after he arrived and reported #730 lost."

Sonny was thinking the same thing. It looked like Lance passed his fob, #729, to the two men to use in accessing the building undetected. Sharon obviously had fob #730 that Lance gave her to use for their rendezvous at the condo. Lance probably wanted to disassociate himself from the second fob by immediately reporting it lost and getting a new one. Perhaps the two large men left #729 behind for Lance in the condo when they exited, since they wouldn't be needing it any longer. He was unsure about what happened to #730 after Sharon used it that evening. It seemed clear to Sonny that whatever initially happened to Sharon that night, happened inside Lance's condo. While he may not have gotten his hands dirty, Lance was just as guilty of causing Sharon's death as the two men who likely abducted her and killed her in the desert.

Sonny thanked Manny for all the help he provided and made good on his promise to arrange for the Dodgers tickets for him. He also made sure that Manny flagged all the important video in the system so that it would be preserved for the police down the road. After receiving some key hard copies of screen grabs depicting the two men and their vehicle along with Sharon's entry, Sonny was on his way. He had plenty of new information to run down now. He was getting closer to the truth.

18

Sonny didn't waste any time in placing a call to RHD to speak with Tim Patrick. He answered on the second ring on his desk phone.

"RHD, Sergeant Patrick. What can I do for you?"

"Tim, this is Sonny. I need a favor. I have a promising lead in the Sharon Summerlin case, but I need to run it out."

"Sure, Tim. What does it involve?"

Sonny proceeded to explain that he was following up on a possible location where Sharon Summerlin may have come across the individuals responsible for her abduction prior to being transported to the desert on the night she was murdered. He detailed the fact that he had a plate from a vehicle that he needed to run and that it would probably come back as a stolen tag or a rental car. He also advised that he texted him a couple of photos of two men that he was trying to identify, in case they were familiar to the LAPD. Sonny provided the plate number to Tim and assured him that if he developed solid information that pointed to a crime being committed in Los Angeles, he would turn everything over so that it could be pursued by the LAPD.

"I will check into it and get back to you as soon as possible. I have to roll out to a scene now where we have a 187, and we also have a high-end smash and grab robbery at a jewelry store that requires my attention," Tim responded.

"Thanks Tim. I know you are busy, and I appreciate your help."

Sonny disconnected the call and drove in the direction of Jim Summerlin's home. He knew that Jim was home from work today and involved in making the final arrangements for Sharon's funeral services. They decided to have a small memorial service attended by family and close friends before her body was cremated in accordance with her wishes. Due to the circumstances of her death, there was a delay in releasing the body for the services. Since the body was now released, they could finish preparations with the funeral home. It would be a closed casket.

Sonny called Jim Summerlin and asked if it would be okay to stop by the house and speak with him privately. Jim told him to come right over. Sonny told him he could be there in half an hour or so.

As he drove toward the Summerlin home, Sonny thought about how he would handle the discussion with Jim Summerlin. It would be a difficult discussion to have, but he had to tell him the truth of what he learned to this point in the investigation to prepare him for what may come down the road.

Sonny also thought more about Lance Frederick. Lance was dirty here; he could feel it. These two goons would not have waltzed into his high-end condo building without his help. It seemed almost certain that Lance was in on the abduction of Sharon Summerlin and perhaps knew the details of her murder in advance. Whether he knew all the details in advance was really a moot point, as he was an accessory to the murder of Sharon Summerlin. Sonny just needed to prove it. He would have to uncover the motive and how the two goons and Lance were connected. One step at a time, Sonny thought.

A short time later, Sonny pulled up outside of Jim's home. There were several vehicles parked in the driveway and two more on the street in front of the home. Most likely relatives that had come in to pay their respects. Sonny walked up to the front gate and announced himself. The gate was unlocked remotely allowing him to enter and walk to the front door. He was met by Jim's younger sister, Susan, and taken inside to the study where Jim was seated behind a mahogany desk. A glass of partially consumed wine was on the desk in front of him.

"Sonny, please come in and have a seat. Can I get you anything to drink?" Jim asked.

"No thanks, I'm fine," Sonny replied before taking a seat in a plush brown chair angled toward the desk. "How are you holding up, Jim?"

"I'm hanging in there but still numb. I cannot believe I am planning my wife's memorial service. I never saw this coming," Jim responded. "Have you developed anything that can help the police?"

"I may have," Sonny began. "What I need to tell you involves circumstantial information and some of my instincts on the case. I am making progress, but need to stress that I haven't tied things together in a way that the police can conclusively act upon. I feel that I am on the right path though. The information I am going to discuss with you must be kept between us for now. We can't take a chance that the individuals responsible might get tipped off. You won't be able to discuss this with your family or anyone else right now. Do you understand?"

Jim shook his head affirmatively signaling that he understood before leaning back in his chair and waiting for Sonny to continue.

"Jim, I told you when you hired me that I would seek out the truth. That is what drives me, learning what really happened to Sharon to try and help you get some kind of closure. I said that I would be straight with you, and I intend to keep that promise."

Jim shifted to the left and seemed to brace himself for where this conversation was going.

"I believe Sharon may have been having an affair," Sonny continued. Jim stared straight ahead without blinking.

"I have been able to trace her movements after she parked her car at LA Live. She went to an upscale condo building within walking distance of the garage. I have her on video entering the building and going up to a residential floor. She does not surface on building video after that, but I suspect that she was abducted from this location and driven out to the desert." Sonny paused.

"Is the person she was seeing responsible for her murder?" Jim responded.

"I believe he was involved in some way but I'm not sure of all of the dynamics yet," Sonny replied.

Jim was floored. He didn't think Sharon would ever cheat on him; it wasn't in her makeup. As he considered what Sonny told him, he had many questions. He also felt a pang of guilt come over him. Had the demands of his career pushed her toward someone else?

Sonny did his best to answer the myriad of questions running through Jim's mind after hearing this gut-wrenching news. He explained to Jim that while he believed that he knew the name of the man Sharon was involved with, he was not yet ready to reveal his identity. He needed to run down several leads first to confirm his suspicions and uncover solid evidence. He also did not yet understand why she was killed but assured Jim that he had a viable investigative path to follow. He also informed Jim that there were some other people that he suspected to be involved in her abduction and murder, but he hadn't identified them yet, although he was confident that he would do so.

"When I put this all together, I will take everything that I have to the police so that the people responsible for her murder are held accountable," Sonny promised.

Jim was stunned. He was deep in thought considering everything that he just heard.

"I know this must be very difficult for you to hear, particularly on top of everything else that has happened and with her services scheduled for tomorrow," Sonny continued. "I must be on the east coast for the next few days on something important that was scheduled before we met. I'm sorry that I won't be able to attend the services but will be working leads on this case and am available to you by phone if you need me."

Jim thanked him and both men stood up and walked toward the door to the study. Before opening the door, Sonny turned toward Jim and looked him in the eye. "We will find out what happened to Sharon and who is responsible, I promise you."

Jim Summerlin put his hand on Sonny's shoulder and nodded solemnly before opening the door and showing him out. He needed to get back to his family and prepare for tomorrow, a task that just became even more arduous.

19

Sonny looked out the window from his seat in first class as the jet was on final approach to Newark Liberty International Airport. He had a great view of the city and the Hudson River as they flew over Met Life Stadium. The late afternoon sun reflected off the tall buildings. The city always looked better from this altitude, he thought. The closer you got, the more you could see the problems and flaws. While he had not been back for some time, he always had that same feeling of coming home. Coming back to his roots.

Although this would be a short visit, he planned to spend some time this afternoon with his mom. Sonny called ahead and arranged for his cousin Rachel to bring her down to the Jersey City waterfront to meet him after he checked into his hotel.

The real reason for his visit was to show support for a former member of his NYPD detective squad, James O'Shea. Jimmy O'Shea was a cop's cop, someone that everyone who ever worked with him came away respecting in a big way. He was smart and conscientious, but what really set him apart was his willingness to go above and beyond to assist his fellow detectives when they needed something on one of their cases. Jimmy never hesitated to help others. That trait saw him rush toward the towers on 9/11. Like many other dedicated police and firefighters, he went there to offer anything that he could do in the search for survivors on that day. Unfortunately, many of those first responders did not wear the proper PPE, personal protective equipment, or respirators to protect them from the combination of building components, chemicals, and jet fuel that contaminated the site of the World Trade Center collapse and hung in the air like a cloud over the entire site. The fire burned for 100 days. Jimmy spent many days working at the "pile" with little rest, breathing in unhealthy air.

Now, later in his life, Jimmy suffered from many maladies including a rare form of cancer. While more than 11,000 other first responders also developed illnesses including more than 3,500 cases of cancer from exposure at the site, most have been recognized as line of duty ailments connected to their prior employment. In Jimmy's case, his insurance claims were denied because he developed his first cancer just under 4 years after exposure, when the latency period was set at 4 years. He later developed several other serious health conditions because of his service. Recently, his health had declined to the point that he lost more than 40 pounds and had trouble standing without assistance. Sonny and many other retired former colleagues of Jimmy had come back to show support for him as he made his final appeal for insurance coverage at a hearing that would take place tomorrow morning.

As the plane stopped and the jet bridge moved to meet the door, Sonny thought of the passengers and crew of United Flight 93, the hijacked flight targeting the US Capitol, that was forced to crash in rural Pennsylvania by the brave actions of those on board. That flight originated here at Newark International on that fateful day. The plane's door opened, and he drifted back to the present. Sonny grabbed his carry-on bag and made a beeline to the air train to connect with a New Jersey Transit train to Newark Penn Station. He then jumped on the PATH train to Journal Square and changed trains to head to Exchange Place, right next to his hotel, the Hyatt Regency Jersey

City. Sonny moved seamlessly between rail lines and stations, having used public transit most of his life here in the New York City metro area. He would much rather take the trains and look at the sights than sit in traffic on the highway.

After walking above ground and covering the block to his hotel, he checked in and emerged to find his mom and cousin sitting on a bench overlooking the Hudson River and across at the Freedom Tower and Lower Manhattan. Sonny walked up behind them and gave them a big group hug, with smiles all around. They spent the next few hours walking along the water looking at the yachts anchored nearby and catching up. It was great seeing them, and the time flew by. Sonny promised his mom he would come back soon when he could spend a week in New York and devour some of her home cooking. He bid them farewell and made a quick stop at the hotel to grab his bag before heading to the ferry for the short trip across to Lower Manhattan. He was on his way to meet Detective Nick Parisi from the NYPD Organized Crime Unit in Brooklyn.

When Sonny arrived at Lombardi's Pizza in Little Italy, Nick was already seated with his back to the wall at a table in the rear of the restaurant. Lombardi's is recognized as the first pizzeria in the US, having opened in 1905. Sonny embraced the aroma as soon as he stepped inside. Nothing like some good NYC pizza to get you feeling right, he thought to himself. Sonny and Nick shared a warm exchange before sitting down to dinner.

Nick Parisi was a newly minted detective that joined Sonny's squad two years before Sonny retired. They kept in touch sporadically, but both planned to support Jimmy at the appeal hearing tomorrow. Now, it was Nick that served as the mentor to the young detectives eager to make their mark in the department. Sonny and Nick discussed current cases and what was new in the

NYPD. There was a lot to talk about, and Sonny thoroughly enjoyed it. As their dinner ended, Sonny removed two photos from his bag of the men that were seen at Lance's condo the night that Sharon Summerlin disappeared. He asked Nick if he could run them past some OC investigators to see if their identities could be determined. Sonny wasn't sure but thought there was a good chance they were from New York originally and thought he would cover that base since he was going to be here anyway. Nick took the photos and said he would get them to the right person's desk tonight with a note to run them by the squad and call him first thing tomorrow with any information. Sonny thanked Nick and headed back toward Jersey City to get some rest.

20

Sonny was up early and ran along the streets bordering a canal before crossing over a small bridge and into Liberty State Park. He had the park to himself at this early hour before the sun rose, and it gave him time to reflect on the case and his next steps. He ran toward the Hudson and saw the Statue of Liberty shining in the distance. But closer ahead, Ellis Island stood as the gateway of entry for so many families looking for a better life in a new land. He always enjoyed running here because he could imagine the excitement, anticipation, and fear that must have gripped these new immigrants upon their arrival. The historical significance of this place was immense. So many families can trace their ancestry here. Sonny wished that he could talk to them about their dreams for their families. So much history passed through Ellis Island, including his own history.

The sun was up as he walked and stretched after the run, gazing across at the city. Sonny had lived here most of his life, but the enormity of the buildings was never lost on him. There really isn't anything like New York here in the US. Sonny loved the energy but didn't miss the crush of people or the cold weather here in the winters. He hurried inside, showered, and grabbed a quick breakfast before jumping on the ferry and heading back into the city for the appeal hearing.

Jimmy O'Shea was happy to see so many old friends there to support him. He made sure to say hello to everyone individually. Sonny had the chance to greet him and give him a big hug. Jimmy felt so frail in his arms. Cancer sucks. It wasn't fair that this man, who sacrificed so much for his fellow New Yorkers, was forced to fight so hard just to receive the medical care he rightly deserved. Another victim of the attacks of 9/11, Sonny thought.

After the hearing, Jimmy seemed to be exhausted. He was on oxygen and needed to get home to rest. His two sons, one a firefighter and the other a police officer, were by his side to get him home safely. His wife passed away several years earlier, killed by a drunk driver who ran a red light and struck her car on the driver's side. In some ways, Jimmy never recovered from losing her. She was his rock. His sons stepped in and were very protective of the only parent they had left.

Sonny thought back to a dark night in Brooklyn years earlier when he and Jimmy walked in on a robbery in progress at a local grocery store. In their haste to escape, the two suspects ran in different directions. Jimmy jumped over the counter and slugged one of them with his fist before the guy could get to the door, knocking him out cold. He then handcuffed him to an ice machine while the guy was face down and unconscious on the floor. But Jimmy wasn't done. He ran in the direction Sonny had gone out the back door into the alley in pursuit of the second suspect. Jimmy arrived just in time as Sonny had his hands full rolling around in the street trying to subdue the suspect. The next thing Sonny knew, the guy abruptly stopped fighting him. Sonny looked up to see Jimmy standing over them with a blackjack dangling from his right hand. Jimmy was credited with two knockouts that night. The thought of his friend full of robustness and vigor brought a smile to his face.

When Sonny got out to the street after the hearing concluded, Nick caught up to him to tell him that they made IDs on the two men in the photos Sonny provided. James Antonelli and Francis Orsini were both lower-level members of the Colombo crime family in Brooklyn. They were known to the NYPD, and both had lengthy criminal records for gambling, loan sharking and assault. The working theory was that they may have been involved in a murder in New York a decade earlier that caused them to flee west to Las Vegas. The murder was never solved. They were last known to be working for Tony Bianchi in Vegas.

Sonny thanked Nick for the information. He made a note of both names and hurried back to the ferry. He called Francine on the way and asked her to see if she could change his travel plans so he could head to Las Vegas today instead of flying back to LA tomorrow. He wanted to jump on this new information right away. Francine said she was on it and would call back with what she found within the hour. As the ferry approached Marcus Hook, he received a text from Tim Patrick. The vehicle on camera at Lance's condo was indeed a rental car from Hertz at McCarran Airport in Las Vegas. Sonny felt a shot of adrenaline surge through his body. This made the decision to stop in Vegas even more valuable. He had two solid leads to pursue. He replied to Tim and thanked him for the information and promised to let him know if this became something they needed to follow-up on.

Sonny grabbed an Uber back to the airport. At this time of day, it would be quicker as traffic wouldn't be as much of a problem. Francine had arranged for him to depart at 2 p.m., and he had just enough time to get through security and to the gate. He would have to grab something to eat on board. He was excited to be moving forward again in the case. He needed to continue to connect the pieces and prove who was responsible for Sharon's murder. He felt like the trip to Vegas would answer some very important questions for him.

21

As soon as he landed in Las Vegas, Sonny sent a message to one of his contacts, Pete Rogers, a former FBI agent who was now working in corporate security for a casino. He needed a quick word if Pete could meet with him in person. While he waited for a reply, he headed for Hertz Rental.

When Sonny arrived at the counter, he stood back and watched the workers interact with customers hurriedly trying to book their cars and get on the road to win all the casino's money. As he studied the three employees, he quickly deduced which one provided the best chance of helping him with the assistance that he needed. Sonny tried to position himself so he would end up in this person's queue. Not an exact science, but he caught a break when an older woman in front of him had difficulty finding her driver's license, which allowed his guy to finish his transaction first, just as Sonny made it to the top of the queue. Sonny immediately stepped up to the counter and produced his driver's license for the helpful young man.

"Good afternoon. Can you help me with a rental car for the next two days while I am here in Las Vegas?" Sonny asked.

"Yes Sir! I am happy to assist," came the reply. "Thank you for being a President's Circle member with Hertz."

The young man typed on the computer while explaining that Sonny could choose any car that he wanted in the Gold or President's Circle area in the garage. Sonny thanked him and then lowered his voice and slid his PI license across the counter.

"I need to ask for some help with a missing persons case I am working. I wonder if you could confirm that this vehicle was rented by Hertz here last Monday, May 4?" Sonny retrieved his license and replaced it with a photo of the rear of the car taken from the ground level garage camera at Lance's condo.

When Sonny saw a slight hesitation, he added that he just wanted to be sure that the person made it safely to Las Vegas and that this was just a formality. The helpful attendant was weighing it in his mind and apparently decided that it couldn't do any harm to check. He went back to his computer and ran the registration number through the system.

"Yes, the Toyota Camry was rented here at the airport on May 4. It was returned here the next day before the counter opened." Sonny asked if the car had been rented again since being returned on May 5th. The attendant looked at the computer before responding.

"Well, the car is due for an oil change, so it wasn't returned to the normal rotation yet. As soon as the oil change is completed by our service department, it will be washed and brought to the garage and available to be rented again."

Sonny asked where the vehicles are stored while awaiting service and was informed that they are parked one level below in the Hertz return area. Sonny thanked him and picked up his rental agreement before walking into the garage to select his car.

Before doing so, he took the nearest stairwell down one level to the area described by the attendant. After walking through two rows, he found the Toyota Camry with the correct registration number. Sonny took out his phone and photographed the vehicle from all four sides. He then took closer photographs of the doors, trunk, and tight shots of each tire tread. He peered through the windows and closely examined the trunk lid. Sonny wished he had the key fob to see inside of the trunk, but that would have to wait.

Sonny dialed the number for the Riverside County Sheriff's Department and asked to speak to Detective Stevens. When Stevens picked up, Sonny explained how he came to believe that this rental car may be involved in the homicide of Sharon Summerlin. He told Stevens that the car was returned the next day and had not been rented since. He explained exactly where it was parked and texted a photo of the vehicle that showed the plate and approximate location in the garage. Sonny suggested that Stevens contact Las Vegas Metro and see if they would impound the vehicle to be processed. He sent him photos of the tires so their evidence people could eyeball them against the casts taken of the tire impressions at the crime scene in advance of getting a search warrant for the vehicle. Stevens agreed and thanked him for the lead. Sonny told him he was going to run down some other information while in Las Vegas and would get back to him as soon as he had additional leads for him to pursue.

After picking up his car, Sonny checked his text messages and saw there was a reply from Pete Rogers. Pete would meet him at Eataly in the Park MGM in 30-minutes. Sonny confirmed and headed that way.

Twenty minutes later Sonny was walking on the sidewalk past the T-Mobile Arena on his way to the Park MGM. As he stepped inside the casino, Sonny was reminded of why he liked the Park MGM. Clean air. He could breathe inside this place. Unlike the other casinos, this one was completely smoke free. He didn't understand why others didn't follow suit. Then he remembered what a casino boss had told him years ago at the

Borgata in Atlantic City while he was surveilling a drug dealer on a money run. He told Sonny, "Got to give the people their 'teins'. Nicotine and caffeine. You do that and they will gamble all day and night." Sonny guessed he was right about that.

Sonny walked up the steps and immediately saw all the food options that mimicked Eataly in NYC. It was just getting busy with the early dinner crowd trying to dine before the 7 p.m. shows. He was eyeing up a charcuterie board when he felt a hand on his shoulder.

"Pete, it is good to see you. Thanks for meeting me on short notice. I would have called ahead but I had a change in itinerary due to a case I am working."

"Never a problem, Sonny. I can always spare a few minutes. I don't mind doing so because the casino owns me and I'm seemingly always here on the strip, much to my wife's chagrin."

Sonny pulled out the photographs, now displaying the names of both mob thugs.

"Well, you picked two model citizens to ask about," Pete commented.

Sonny described some of the case to him but focused on the fact that these two may have some connection to it, and asked Pete where he might be able to find them. Since Pete ran the FBI's organized crime investigations in Las Vegas for about a decade, he was infinitely familiar with the local talent, including these two.

"Antonelli and Orsini are two leg breakers from New York that made their way to our fine city following a murder investigation that we believe they are good for but there wasn't enough to tie them to it directly. The mob relocation program must have felt they were good candidates for a change of scenery. They are working for Tony Bianchi. He runs prostitutes, drugs, gambling, and extortion rackets here in town. He is capable of serious violence if it suits his needs. He's been around and doesn't talk on the phone much. Keeps himself insulated as much as possible. He works above a bar he owns called Frank's Place, a few blocks off the strip." Pete gave him the address and Sonny thanked him for the help.

"Be careful around these guys, Sonny. They aren't to be trifled with."

Sonny thanked his friend again and told him he would buy dinner the next time he was in town or when Pete came out to LA.

"I will look forward to it," Pete said as he walked back toward the casino floor.

22

Sonny went back to the garage and picked-up the rental car. He crossed over the strip and onto Audrie Street running parallel to head north. Sonny followed the directions on his phone and worked his way over to the side street where the restaurant/bar that Pete had described was located. He pulled into a small lot across the street in front of a nail salon, and parked in a spot facing the restaurant where he had a clear view of the main entrance. Sonny made himself comfortable since he didn't know how long he would be sitting there.

The sun had set, and Sonny felt less conspicuous with the cloak of darkness that enveloped the city. Even though there were plenty of lights all around, the shadows provided a sense of anonymity for him. He had been sitting there for about an hour and forty-five minutes when he finally saw Jimmy and Frank exit through the main entrance and walk across the parking lot to a black Cadillac sedan parked in a handicapped spot. Sonny started his car and slowly backed up and eased toward the exit, stopping short behind a parked car, and waited to see which direction the Cadillac would go.

The Cadillac, with Jimmy at the wheel, pulled out and turned left in front of oncoming traffic. Sonny heard the horns blare as he pulled out behind the cluster of cars that the Cadillac had cut off. After closing the distance, he was able to sit back and easily identify their car because of the distinctive taillights. A few minutes later, the Cadillac turned right and went three blocks before pulling into the parking lot of a strip club and parking near the entrance. They got out and entered the club.

Sonny slowly passed by the strip club and pulled into the parking lot next door. He quickly parked and made his way into the strip club lot. He walked toward the front door but slowed to glance inside the Cadillac. The windows had dark tinting, and this made it difficult to see anything inside the car. Sonny continued to the entrance and went inside.

It took a moment for Sonny's eyes to adjust to the lighting inside of the club. Once he did so, he took in the layout. There was a large stage in the center where naked women were dancing with bar top seating all around. There were tables set up along the walls around the perimeter, which were not well lit. On the back wall, there were what appeared to be private rooms along with a service door and a set of stairs leading to an office upstairs. Sonny decided to take a seat at the bar where he could see most of the room including the upstairs portion and ordered a drink.

Inside of the surveillance room in a small office upstairs, the guy running the cameras noticed some things that drew his attention. The cameras he controlled provided a view of both the outside and inside of the club. He turned to his partner and asked him to go next door and get Jimmy. When Jimmy stepped inside, he proceeded to show him a few video snippets that he had queued up on a large screen.

"The guy here sitting at the bar looks like he may have followed you guys to the club. He looks like a cop or something. Here you can see his vehicle slow down as you pull into the lot. He parks next door and walks over. Here you can see him stop and try to look inside your car. He appears to be more interested in the club layout than the girls right in front of him."

Jimmy took it all in before responding. "Send someone over to see who this guy is. Let me know what we find out."

A short time later, Sonny saw a tall, muscular, light skinned black guy wearing a wife beater T-shirt and a ponytail walk toward him at the bar. He stopped right in front of Sonny and told him that he needed to have a word with him, and asked Sonny to follow him back to the office. Sonny stood up and followed him around the bar to a door along the back wall leading into a narrow hallway. As soon as he entered the hallway, he saw a flash behind him, and another guy hit him hard from behind with a forearm to the back of his neck just as Ponytail spun around and kneed him in the gut. The guy behind him drove him into the wall while grabbing and pinning his left arm behind him. He held him in place as Ponytail ripped his wallet out of his pocket. He looked inside and saw Sonny's PI credentials.

"You a little out of your neighborhood, bitch. What the fuck are you investigating in our club, motherfucker?"

"I'm working on a divorce case with a cheating spouse," Sonny tried to get out with his face still firmly pressed against the wall. Ponytail didn't seem to be impressed by his explanation.

"That's some weak ass shit. You didn't ask no permission to come up in here. If I ever catch your dumb ass in here again, bitch, you gonna get hurt."

At that moment, the guy behind him whipped him around against the opposite wall before driving him like a football blocking sled at full speed down the hallway and through the exit door at the other end and out into the rear lot. Sonny hit the asphalt hard and rolled onto his right side. Ponytail stepped outside and threw Sonny's wallet into his face while he was on the ground.

"Now take your unwelcome ass back to LA, bitch." Ponytail and his partner went back inside and slammed the door.

Sonny rolled over and got to his feet and brushed himself off. He put his wallet back into his pocket and checked to see that he still had his phone, and that it wasn't broken. Sonny walked around the back of the club and crossed the parking lot on his way back to the rental car. He hoped that by not fighting them, they would believe his story that he was just working on a divorce case. Sonny unlocked the car and headed to his hotel to take a shower, regroup, and get some sleep. He would be back at it first thing tomorrow. He was obviously on the right track. That much he was sure of.

23

Lance Frederick was starting to feel more than a little unsettled. Even though it had been a few days since he was "ambushed" by the private investigator at the mayor's event, he had become obsessed with what this man might know. Who hired him and what was he looking for? Obviously, he had somehow connected him to Sharon Summerlin. He did not know how that was possible, as he went to great lengths to keep the relationship a secret. She promised not to tell anyone about them. Did she betray him yet again? He wished that he had never had anything to do with her. He had to find a way to limit any potential damage this could cause.

Because he had 45-minutes before he needed to attend an internal planning meeting, Lance had some time to reconsider everything. What was the biggest threat to him? He didn't kill anyone, so how could they try to pin that on him? He never knew exactly what they were planning. All he did was provide his key fob. And nobody would ever know that. She was killed out in the desert. They wouldn't be able to connect her to his condo. After all, Lance had the perfect alibi for that evening. And he didn't go back to the condo until the following afternoon to report his key fob as missing. Anyone could have had his key fob. How would he know?

The money he received for steering construction contracts to mob related businesses controlled by Tony Bianchi would be difficult to trace. In fact, both he and Bianchi had put in a few layers to separate themselves from each other. Lance helped to manipulate the bid process to make it appear that the successful bid companies won the contracts on the merits and for no other reason. There were some campaign finance violations and permit issues as well, but again, they were well hidden, and he had distanced himself from those transactions.

Maybe he was overreacting. His friends in Las Vegas were certainly not going to give him up, so it really came down to what the private investigator could prove. Maybe one of her girlfriends had shot her mouth off, but what did that prove? It was her word against his, and there was nothing concrete linking him to Sharon. Lance was very careful to avoid meeting her in public. Yes, the more he thought about it, maybe he was in a better position than he previously thought he was. He just needed to keep a low profile, and all of this would blow over and he would continue living in the manner to which he had become accustomed.

However, to be on the safe side, he should probably report what happened with the private investigator to Tony. It would be risky not to tell him. The man had a hair trigger and went from zero to one hundred in a matter of seconds. Lance did not want to do anything to get on his bad side, and being seen as withholding important information was a not a risk worth taking. Also, Tony and his men had the ability to get someone to adjust their behavior. Perhaps by telling Tony about the encounter, he would intercede and convince the PI to reconsider nosing around in something that was none of his business. Yes, telling Tony had much more upside than risk.

Lance went over and closed the door to his office. He removed the burner phone from his briefcase and dialed the emergency number he had been provided. The same one that he called a little over a week ago that set all this in motion. After several rings, a voice answered and told him to hold on. Then Tony answered.

"I was at an event last week and a private investigator ambushed me and started asking questions about Sharon. I told him I didn't know who he was referring to, but he wouldn't take no for an answer. I finally cut him off and said he was mistaken and that I had to get back to work. I didn't give him anything," Lance reported.

Tony asked him to describe the PI. Lance did so and Tony conferred with someone in the background before coming back on the line. "We will handle it. You just keep your mouth shut."

"Of course, whatever you say."

Then the call disconnected, and he turned off the phone and put it back in his briefcase. He hoped that he had seen the last of the private investigator. He wanted to forget about Sharon Summerlin and put everything behind him. She got what she deserved.

Lance stood up and closed his iPad while he walked to the door. It was time to compartmentalize and get back to performing his job in the same way that he always did.

24

Tony disconnected the call and turned his attention to Jimmy and Frank. "So, tell me what happened with this guy and what we know about him?"

Jimmy replied and described the events of last evening at the club and how the guy came to their attention on the surveillance video. He told Tony how a couple of the guys slapped him around and found out he was a PI from LA.

"What the fuck was he doing at our club?"

"We don't know for sure, but he could have followed me and Frank inside. He showed up right after we got there," Jimmy answered. "Said he was working on a divorce case with a cheating spouse or something."

"We don't know who this dipshit is working for, and I don't like the fact that he's from LA and just happens to fall out of the fucking sky and into our club right after the other thing. On top of that, before he ends up here, he is asking questions about Lance's girlfriend. I don't believe in coincidences."

Jimmy asked, "You want us to do something?"

"Yeah, I do. I want both of you to take your fat asses back down there and find out who the fuck he is working for and what the fuck he is working on. I want to know what he knows about Lance and if he can connect us in any way. Then we will decide how it gets handled. Now get moving."

"You got it, Boss," Jimmy replied while he and Frank stood up and headed for the door.

25

Jim Summerlin was beginning to become depressed. The enormity of the murder of his wife was now becoming difficult to bear. When he first learned that she had been murdered, he was numb. He found a way to continue with the support of family and friends. Now that the funeral services had concluded and extended family went back to their homes and lives, he felt alone. The person or persons responsible for taking her away from him were still out there. They had not been held accountable for what they had done, for wrecking his life and their future together. The fact that Sharon may have had an affair that put in motion the twisted and evil actions that resulted in her death, did not overshadow how Jim remembered her, nor did it dull his profound feelings of loss and sadness.

Jim went back to work two days after her services. He did so because he felt it was expected of him since the studio business would not slow down because of the loss of his wife. Also, he did not know how he would cope with being at home alone for days at a time knowing that Sharon was never coming home again.

Jim heard something and looked up to see his assistant standing in front of his desk with several folders containing information on potential acquisitions that the studio was considering. He thanked her and put the files on his desk but didn't have the strength to read them at this moment. Instead, he focused on the silver framed photo on the corner of his desk. It was a photo of him with Sharon attending a show at the

Hollywood Bowl last year. Her smile was amazing, and he remembered how she made him feel when they had the chance to be together. His work often intruded, but it was also his work that was responsible for them ever meeting in the first place. Jim missed her more than he could ever express. He just felt very sad and somewhat helpless now. These were not emotions that he had experienced before. Jim was always upbeat and in control, leading others in a way that inspired their confidence in him, trusting in his steady hand at the helm. Right now, he didn't feel like that guy at all.

Jim's assistant buzzed his phone. "Mr. Summerlin, Sonny Romano is on the line. Should I transfer him back to you?"

"Yes, send him back," he replied.

Jim picked up and thanked Sonny for calling.

"How are you holding up, Jim?"

"I'm doing the best that I can. Do you know more about who killed Sharon or why she was murdered?"

Sonny began by telling Jim that he was in Las Vegas following up on leads that were developed in the past few days.

"We are making progress. As I alluded to previously, I know that Sharon visited a condo building near LA Live the night that she disappeared. The person that I believe she was seeing owns a unit in that building. The building is about a 10-minute walk from where Sharon parked her car. I was able to review security footage that shows her in the lobby and taking an elevator up to the floor where his condo is located. I do not think that he was there that night but may have led her to believe that he would be."

"I have also uncovered evidence that two men associated with organized crime in Las Vegas were there that night. I think that they may have been waiting for Sharon when she arrived and overpowered her. I have reviewed video showing them leaving the floor pushing a luggage cart that I believe Sharon was concealed on. They went to the parking garage and left the condo building heading east."

"I was able to trace the vehicle here to Las Vegas. It is a rental car that was rented at McCarran Airport on the Monday afternoon she disappeared and returned to the airport in Las Vegas during the early morning hours of Tuesday, May 5, before the Hertz counter opened for the day. I have photos of the car and have involved law enforcement authorities in Riverside County and here in Las Vegas to have the car impounded and searched. There were tire impressions discovered at the scene in the desert where Sharon was found that can be compared to the tread pattern on the rental car. Also, it is possible that other trace evidence may be found when the police search the car. All of that is happening now and I hope to learn more soon," Sonny said and then stopped to pause in case Jim had any questions for him.

"I don't understand. Why were these men from Las Vegas involved? Organized crime? It doesn't make any sense to me," Jim said.

"I'm trying to find the connection between the man she was seeing and the organized crime figures from Las Vegas. There must be a connection and I intend to find it. The person they work for is a mobster named Tony Bianchi. He runs several types of criminal rackets here in Las Vegas. These are serious criminals. They wouldn't be involved unless there was a financial incentive for them to do so."

"But how does any of this involve Sharon? Surely, she was not involved in organized crime."

"It is possible that she may have seen or overheard something that could threaten their criminal scheme in some way. She may have been killed because of that."

"They need to pay for what they did to Sharon. All of them. Whoever was involved," Jim stated.

"I will do everything that I can to uncover the truth and provide it to law enforcement so that those responsible can be prosecuted and sent to prison for what they did. You have my word. For now, please keep our discussion between us. I will continue to work this and plan to be back in LA later today. I will be in touch when I have new information to share with you."

"Thank you, Sonny. I know you are doing everything that you can to solve Sharon's murder. I appreciate it, I really do. Things are just a bit overwhelming for me right now."

"Jim, for what it's worth, I have found evidence that indicates that Sharon was going to break it off with him on the night that she was killed."

There was silence for a time before Jim responded. "Do you think that may have played a role in her murder?"

"No, I don't think he knew that she was going break it off. I think the abduction and murder were set in motion in advance." Sonny paused before continuing. "Hang in there Jim. We will see this through." Sonny then disconnected the call. He felt a great deal of empathy for Jim. He was clearly still suffering very much.

Sonny stood up and stretched out his back and neck. He was sore from the little dance class last night at the strip club, but he had no other choice than to absorb it if he wanted them to believe that he was just a PI working on a cheating spouse divorce case. However, he would have enjoyed mopping the floor with Ponytail and his friend. Maybe some other time. Sonny wasn't sure that they bought his story but was hoping that he didn't draw the attention of Jimmy and Frank. He needed more information before going to the police to have them all confronted directly. He wanted to operate in the background for as long as possible.

26

After finishing the call with Jim, Sonny had an idea and decided to reach back out to Pete with a request since he was still in Las Vegas. He called the number and was surprised when Pete picked up after the second ring.

"Good morning, Sonny. How did you make out last night?"

"Well, I think I made an impression, but it was my face on some drywall in a hallway," Sonny replied.

"Are you okay? Do you need anything?"

"I'm fine, Pete. I think they just wanted to send me a message. I tried to play it like I was working on a divorce case, but the fact that they targeted me for extra attention makes me think that they may have connected me to some of my moves back in LA. Time will tell, I guess. But that's not why I called. I was wondering if I could get some advice about another aspect of the case involving the guy we spoke of yesterday."

"Sure thing. What can I help you with?"

Sonny explained that he was interested in identifying the companies owned by Tony Bianchi. He wanted to determine the types of legitimate businesses that he was involved with. Sonny knew that the FBI needed to conduct this type of background routinely when assessing a criminal target and thought that Pete might be able to steer him in the right direction.

Pete said, "I'll tell you what, if you can give me a few minutes, I will reach out to a friend of mine at the Nevada Department of State. He was helpful to us when I was working cases here in Las Vegas. He is adept at making the connections between business holdings and if he is available this week, I'm sure that he wouldn't mind assisting you. The information that you are looking for is public information, so it's not as if he is providing access to anything confidential. All the information is available if you know how to search for it online. He will be able to greatly reduce the time necessary to collect it. Let me reach out to him and I will call you right back either way. He works out of a state office building here in Las Vegas. When is your flight back to LA?"

"I don't leave until around 2 p.m.," Sonny replied.

"Good. Let me see what I can find out."

Pete disconnected the call and Sonny jumped in the shower so he wouldn't be wasting any time. Fifteen minutes later his phone rang, and Pete had good news for him.

"The guy's name is Steve Fleming. He has some time this morning if you can get to his office by 11 a.m."

Sonny thanked him and Pete gave him the address for the office and Steve's mobile number.

"Shoot him a text when you are downstairs at his building. He will come down and escort you up to his office."

"I owe you my friend," Sonny said.

"Yes, you're now in the hole for two dinners at the restaurants of my choosing. You better get going. Let me know if there is anything else that you need here in the desert."

"You got it. I really appreciate it," Sonny said before disconnecting the call.

Sonny used the map GPS on his phone to see how long it would take to get to the office. He had enough time to finish getting dressed and pack his bag before checking out and grabbing the rental car from the garage. No time for breakfast. He would try to grab something at the airport before his flight.

Twenty-five minutes later, Sonny was standing in the lobby of the Nevada government building housing Department of State offices in Las Vegas. He texted Steve Fleming and told him he was downstairs in the lobby. Steve replied that he would be right down to get him.

A few minutes went by before a man in his early to mid-forties stepped out of the elevator and introduced himself as Steve Fleming. He was wearing a bolo tie with a turquoise stone in the shape of an arrowhead. They exchanged pleasantries before heading up to the 7th floor where Steve's office was located.

Sonny pulled out a sheet of paper from his bag containing a photo along with the name Antonio "Tony" Bianchi. He also had noted the names and addresses of the bar/restaurant and strip club that he believed may be businesses that were owned by Bianchi here in Las Vegas.

Steve Fleming took the sheet of paper and placed it off to the side of his computer and started to type. After about ten minutes, he finished and said that he was able to find 25 or so businesses that Bianchi either owned or held some sort of corporate position in the State of Nevada.

"There are a few bars and restaurants, a couple of laundromats and a spa. But he is also involved with several construction companies, a trucking firm, and several self-storage locations. I sent each one over to the printer so you would be able to review each company, its latest statement of information filed with the state, and the listing of corporate officers. It is possible that some of these companies may also have locations in other states, but our system won't show me that sort of information."

Sonny was excited to review the reports. He would do so on the plane. Even though this might seem to be mundane, he was interested identifying potential companies that Bianchi was involved with that may have bid on contracts with the City of Los Angeles. He needed to know what names to look for when he obtained the information he would seek back in LA. Maybe he could find a link between Bianchi and Lance Frederick.

"Thank you for helping me out with this, Steve. You probably saved me a day of work," Sonny said while giving him one of his business cards. "Let me know if you get down to LA and we can grab lunch."

Steve had assembled a file about an inch thick with the printed material enclosed and handed it to Sonny before they both exited the office to go back to the lobby.

Sonny put the folder inside his bag and was on his way to return his rental car at the airport. As he made his way to the rental return, he glanced toward the level where the rental car that he believed was used to transport Sharon had been parked. He hoped that the forensic examination of it would yield important evidence linking it to her murder.

After dropping off his car and clearing through security, Sonny stopped at Jamba Juice to grab a PB Banana Protein smoothie with soy. It was one of his go to favorites that had the added benefit of being able to be consumed while he walked to his gate. Soon, he was settled in his seat on the plane and immediately took out the folder on Tony Bianchi to read quickly on the short hour and fifteen-minute flight back to LA.

27

It seemed like he had just started reviewing the file when Sonny felt the wheels touch down at LAX. It was a quick flight, but he made good progress on his examination of the material supplied by Steve Fleming. He still had more to read, but he highlighted several businesses and made notes in the file for later. After exiting the plane, Sonny called Francine back at the office to check in with her.

"Sonny, how did things go in Las Vegas?"

Sonny brought her up to date on the rental car and his surveillance of Jimmy and Frank which led to the strip club. He also informed her of the information that he received this morning from the Nevada Department of State.

"It sounds like diverting to Las Vegas was definitely worth it," Francine added.

"It was. I wanted to let you know that I am going to go straight downtown from here. I want to try to see if I can catch Darlene and file some FOIA requests to cross reference against the information I collected earlier today."

FOIA was a general acronym for the Freedom of Information Act that Sonny hoped would further illuminate any potential connections between Tony Bianchi and Lance Frederick. In California it was often referred to as a CPRA request. Sonny had become friendly with one of the employees at the city that helped to comply with California Public Records Act requests. The city had 10 days to make a determination in response to a formal request. Sonny hoped that he might be able obtain some information today in advance of receiving the PDF from the city after the normal process ran its course.

"After I run downtown, I plan to head over to my condo to unpack. I'm going to come into the office tonight after the traffic dies down. Can you leave me the information on Tony Bianchi that you were able to put together before you leave for the day?"

"No problem. I started working on it when I received your text this morning. Also, there are a few files for you to review on other cases. I will leave them on your desk as well."

"Thanks Francine. I will see what progress I make tonight and follow-up with you in the morning. Thanks for the assist here."

"You don't have to thank me, just doing my job. Don't stay too late. You probably could use some rest."

Sonny disconnected the call and used the freeway to head downtown. It was risky but he hoped he could make it before traffic volume started to pick up for the early evening rush. In LA, people worked all different hours to try to reduce their commute times. It made planning to get somewhere quickly a bit more difficult to predict. He steered the Tesla into the HOV lane as soon as he entered the 105 freeway. He would take it east before turning north on the 110 freeway. Thirty minutes later, he dropped down off the freeway onto North Figueroa to take surface streets to a garage near City Hall.

Sonny hustled from the garage over to City Hall and to the department where he would file the official CPRA request. He spotted Darlene and approached her at the counter.

"Darlene, I need to ask a favor," Sonny began.

Darlene replied, "Why am I not surprised to hear you say those words?"

"Fair point. I came straight here from the airport so I didn't have the time to pick-up your favorite cupcakes from Magnolia Bakery, but I promise I will make it up to you."

"You better. We close in an hour so you better hurry and tell me what you need."

Sonny went on to explain that he would file a written CPRA request for all contracts awarded by the City of Los Angeles for $500,000 or more since the new mayoral administration took over. However, he knew that he wouldn't receive the written response for close to two weeks and was hoping that she would do a quick pre-check and apprise him verbally of the company names and amounts that were in the system and would be part of the more detailed written response he received later.

Darlene considered the request before responding. "Give me 30-minutes. That will also give you plenty of time to walk over to Mwokaji Cakery a couple of blocks away on Los Angeles Street and bring me back a couple of chocolate cupcakes. Pick out the ones that look the best. When you get back, I should have something for you."

Sonny did as he was told and hustled over to Mwokaji Cakery and picked out two of the most delicious looking chocolate cupcakes in the entire place. They were wrapped up for him and he was out the door and on his way back to Darlene. Downtown was beginning to empty out as 4:30 p.m. quickly approached. When he arrived, Sonny saw Darlene hold up her hand as if to say 'wait' and he stopped and sat on a chair where he had a good view of her work area.

A few minutes later, she motioned for him to come back to the window. "Okay. I found 20 entries that match the criteria you asked for during the first 18-months of the new administration. That is all that I had time for right now, but you should get everything in your written request after it goes through the review process. This is a pretty standard request, so I would think it should be turned around in 10 days or so."

Sonny took out his notepad and began writing the names and amounts of the contracts as Darlene read them off. She couldn't print them for him, as this would circumvent the normal process and could get her in trouble. After they finished, Sonny slid the bag across the counter to her. She opened it and inhaled deeply.

"You did good Sonny!"

"I'm glad I picked the right ones," he replied. Then he closed his notebook and thanked her again for her help. He headed back outside and toward the garage. Sonny knew that he didn't have the full list, but hoped when he compared what he had to the list of companies from Nevada, that something would match up to give him a place to start. He would lay everything out in the office tonight and see if anything matched up. There had to be a connection to Lance. He just needed to find it.

28

Rush hour was in full swing when he exited the parking garage. Sonny decided to take surface streets instead of being stuck in traffic on the freeway. It still took 45-minutes for him to get home. He left all the files locked in the trunk and took his bag up to the condo to unpack.

Sonny decided to take a power walk around part of the marina, then across the lagoon bridge and along the beach. This would give him time to think and allow traffic to thin out before heading to the office. The sun was beginning to dip in the late afternoon sky but still reflected brightly off the ocean. He picked up his pace as he headed up the beach.

His phone rang and he saw that the caller ID showed Riverside County. Sonny answered the call and was greeted by Detective Stevens.

"Sonny, Detective Stevens from Riverside. Do you have a minute?"

"Sure thing. Just got back from Las Vegas this afternoon. How are you making out with the investigation?"

"Well, we were able to work with Las Vegas Metro to obtain a search warrant for the vehicle. We sent an evidence technician and another detective up to assist with the search and chain of custody issues. We are waiting for several items that were submitted to the lab for examination. However, the preliminary comparison of the tire impressions from the murder scene looks to be a match with the rental car tires."

"That is great news," Sonny responded. "That will go a long way to connecting our guys from Vegas to the crime scene."

"I agree. This will be supported by the video evidence you located at the condo near where the victim parked her car."

Sonny went on to explain his recent interaction with the OC figures in Las Vegas after reporting the location of the rental car. He also informed Stevens that he planned to review business records this evening to see if he could find any potential connections from the mob to Lance Frederick. He promised to report anything that he found that might support a connection.

They agreed to catch-up soon and disconnected the call. Sonny reflected on the tire impressions and what it could mean for the case. These guys were observed at the condo where the victim was last seen alive. And the car they left in was tied to the scene of the murder. That was pretty strong evidence of their involvement. Now, he needed to tie Lance into the conspiracy and find a way to bridge to Tony Bianchi, the person that most likely ordered the murder of Sharon Summerlin.

The case was beginning to come into focus. There was still much to do to put this in front of a jury and obtain a conviction of all those responsible for Sharon's murder. He was excited and he felt like they were making good progress. Sonny was now energized to get into the office and sift through the documents he collected today. He needed to find the connection between Lance and the mob in Vegas. He went upstairs to get cleaned up and grab a quick bite to eat before going to the office. The positive energy and optimism propelled him forward.

29

Jimmy eased the Cadillac sedan into the parking lot of the small shopping plaza across from the building that housed Sonny's office. He located a parking spot that provided a view of the front of the building from across the street. It was just after 6 p.m. and they wondered if Sonny was inside his office. They really didn't know if he was even back in LA. For all they knew, he was still in Las Vegas.

"Take a walk across the street and go through the parking garage down below and get the lay of the land," Jimmy said to Frank.

"I'll give it a look but if he is there, we don't want him to know that we're here," Frank replied. "Let me see what I can find out."

Frank opened the passenger door and walked over to the crosswalk at the next intersection. He crossed the street and ducked into the parking garage. Inside, he saw that most of the parking spaces were empty this time of day. The spots were numbered, so there was no way to tell which tenants were assigned to each spot. He assumed there must be some sort of allotment of some kind. Frank moved toward the elevator bank and used the stairs to the right to walk up to the lobby on the 1st floor. Inside the lobby, he saw a few doors with nameplates of businesses. None of these corresponded to Sonny Romano in any way. Frank walked over to the framed business directory hanging next to the elevator. There it was. 'Sonny Romano, Private Investigations, Suite 206.'

Frank took his time walking up to the second floor. He had observed a camera mounted high in the lobby that was aimed at the front door entrance from the street and most likely picked up the stairwell entry and the elevator door inside the lobby. When he reached the second floor, Frank saw that there were name plates on doors going both ways with corresponding suite numbers mounted underneath. Suite 206 was to his right at the end of the hall. Frank stopped to listen for a minute but did not hear anything in the hallway from any of the offices located on this floor. He slowly walked toward Suite 206 and saw that the door was closed and appeared to be locked with no light coming out from under the door. Frank thought that perhaps nobody was inside, but he couldn't be sure. He took a quick look at the lock and felt that they would be able to defeat it without having to be obvious and bust in by shattering the door frame and leaving a telltale mess. Now that he knew where the office was located inside, they could observe the windows on the exterior of the building for any sign that somebody was working inside the office. Frank walked back down the steps to the parking garage before exiting and walking back across the street to the Cadillac.

"Well, what does it look like?" Jimmy asked.

"The office is on the second floor on the east side of the building. It appears to be locked and empty. If we can park the car in the lot across the street on the right side, we should be able to see any windows that he has and maybe get a sense if he is in there," Frank responded.

Jimmy pulled out of the lot and executed a U-turn at the intersection and pulled into the first lot east of Sonny's building. They could see two windows with the shades partially closed but could not determine if any lights were on inside since it was still daylight outside. They decided to go and grab dinner somewhere nearby and come back after dark to watch the place before breaking in.

At 6:40 p.m., Sonny pulled into the garage and parked in his first assigned spot. He used the steps to go up to the second floor and unlocked his office before closing and locking the door behind him. Sonny turned on the lights and went into his office. He drew both shades closed before taking a seat at his desk and unloading the files onto the desktop.

Before getting started on the files, Sonny went through the mail that Francine left on his desk as well as the new files in his inbox to get an idea what he needed to act on while he was there. After handling everything and jotting a few quick notes for Francine, he was ready to get started.

Sonny placed the business information from Nevada on the right side of the desk and his notes on the city contracts more than $500,000 that were awarded during the first 18-months of the new mayoral administration on the left side. He separated the business information by type, beginning with the ones most likely to result in a contract that the City of Los Angeles might award. After about twenty minutes, Sonny found something of interest. Twelve construction contracts that were bid within 6-months of the new administration taking over were awarded to several different contractors. One of the contractors was a construction company from Nevada where Tony Bianchi was listed in the business filings as the COO. This particular company had been awarded contracts on three different projects undertaken by the city. The contracts were to perform part of the work on each contract while other firms were selected to complete the remaining portions of each project. It appeared that

Bianchi's company received the bid to do both demolition and asbestos removal, as well as new construction and paving. The total amount of these contracts was more than $2.3 million when added together. Not a trivial amount of city tax dollars by any means.

While this discovery did not conclusively prove a connection between the Mayor's Chief of Staff and the Las Vegas mob, it was something that would need to be investigated thoroughly. If Lance had rigged the process to steer the contract awards to companies owned or operated by Tony Bianchi in return for something of value, then there would be a solid basis upon which the criminal conspiracy that led to the murder of Sharon Summerlin could be built. If Sharon had somehow discovered what Lance and Bianchi were up to, she may have been killed to tie up that potential loose end. He hoped the police would be able to prove that both Lance and Tony Bianchi took part in Sharon's murder.

After scouring all the other records, Sonny did not find any other potential connections. He knew that he may find others in the additional data that the city would send to him after researching and approving his request, but at least he had something tangible that could be investigated now. Sonny would have to give some thought to how the complex jurisdictional issues involved could be navigated to serve both the murder investigation and any other potential criminal offenses that may have been committed. He closed the files and left them in the folders on his desk before turning off the lights and locking the front door. He thought he needed to go home and get some rest. He planned to be back first thing tomorrow morning. It was almost 9 p.m., and by the time Sonny got home, it would be time to hit the sack. He needed to consider his next moves in the case.

30

When they returned an hour later, they immediately noticed that the blinds on the east facing side of the second-floor office were now closed and light was emanating from inside the office. A quick check of the garage by Frank disclosed that only two cars were parked inside, and one was new. A Tesla Model 3 that Frank had not seen on his earlier recon of the garage. They took up a position where they could see both the windows of Sonny's office and the entry to the parking garage.

At about 9 p.m., the lights in the office went off. They waited and approximately two minutes later, they observed the garage arm come up and a Tesla pull out before turning west. It was dark and the windows were tinted, so they were unable to see inside the vehicle. Frank jotted down the plate number in case they needed it in the future.

"Looks like our boy is done for the evening," Jimmy remarked. "Let's give it fifteen minutes to be sure he isn't coming back before we hit the place." Frank nodded his approval, and they sat in silence and waited for the time to pass.

When they felt certain that Sonny wasn't going to return to the office, they got out and made their way through the garage and up to the second floor. They would take the chance that the office wasn't alarmed but would try to get in and out quickly just in case. They both pulled out gloves from their pockets and Jimmy stood watch while shielding Frank as he went to work on the lock. A few minutes later, the door was unlocked, and they moved quickly inside. There was no audible alarm, but they couldn't be sure that a silent alarm or motion triggered alarm wouldn't be activated by their movements inside. They did not turn on the lights but used a small flashlight to scan the interior of the office area. After rapidly moving past the reception area, they entered Sonny's office in the back.

Frank went to check the filing cabinets, but they were locked. Because they did not have the time to mess with them, he opened the closet door to look inside while Jimmy went over to the desk. Jimmy conducted a fast check of the drawers but didn't find anything that looked too important. The investigative case files must be in the file cabinets or on his computer, Jimmy thought. The desktop computer was protected by a password, and as he was considering whether they should take it with them, Jimmy saw a file folder on the right side of the desk that was about an inch thick. Frank had joined him and was rifling through some manila folders that were found lying in an inbox tray on top of the desk.

Frank looked up and noticed that Jimmy was engrossed in reading something he found in the thick folder.

"Our businesses in Vegas are all through this. And it looks like amounts are highlighted from the contracts we got from the city. This fucking guy is connecting the dots here," Jimmy said.

"Tony isn't going to be happy. We need to tell him right away," Frank responded.

Jimmy used his phone to take a couple of photos before putting the file back like he found it. They retraced their steps back to the front door. Frank checked the hallway and gave the all clear sign before they both exited and hustled down the steps and out of the garage in case they triggered an alarm that would result in a police response. They got back into the Cadillac and exited the parking lot, looking to get away from the office building before stopping to call Tony.

Tony Bianchi was just finishing dessert after a late dinner at one of his favorite spots just off the strip. One of his guys came over to the table and apologized for interrupting his dinner.

"I got a call from Jimmy. He says he needs to talk to you right away," he said.

"Tell him I will call him in 20-minutes from the car," Tony directed.

The guy retreated from the table and delivered the message to Jimmy.

Tony finished his meal and considered what Jimmy wanted to tell him. He sent them down to LA to find out what the PI was up to and what he knew. It was not a positive development that Jimmy felt the need to speak to him so soon after they arrived.

When Tony was in the car in a secure environment, he pulled out a new burner phone and called Jimmy. "What do you need to tell me that couldn't wait?"

Jimmy replied, "Boss, we got into his office after he left and found files listing our businesses in Las Vegas along with the amounts of the city contracts that we got through Lance. It was all laid out and highlighted with handwritten notes and shit."

There was a pause before Tony responded. "Doesn't mean he can prove anything, but it isn't good. I need to consider a couple of things but will call you early tomorrow morning. Be ready to answer and we will address this." Tony hung up.

Jimmy put the phone down and turned to Frank. “He’s not happy. He wants us to be ready for instructions tomorrow morning. Let’s go get a hotel room and some sleep.”

31

Sonny was awake at 4:15 a.m. but remained in bed thinking about the case for a half hour longer. The potential connection between Lance and the mob was a promising possibility, but he still did not have any proof at this point that there was an underlying criminal conspiracy that formed the motive for Sharon's murder. If however, there were financial records that showed that Lance received kickbacks in exchange for steering the lucrative contracts to the mob, that could be used to prove motive. That in combination with the video evidence that Sharon went to his condo and was likely abducted before being murdered in the desert, would go a long way to potentially convicting him at least as an accessory to her murder.

Sonny was starting to believe that perhaps he should take a run at Lance and try to convince him that his only hope was to cooperate with the police now. Doing so would directly implicate Tony Bianchi and his crew in Sharon's murder. Lance would still go to prison, but his cooperation in testifying against the man who ordered the hit would likely mean that he would not spend the rest of his life behind bars. This could be his only chance of helping himself before he ultimately went down with the rest of them for life.

Sonny decided to jog down to the beach and do calisthenics on the fixed apparatus before running through a series of katas. Then he could jog back. He would be finished before anyone was in his way since it was only approaching 5 a.m. on a Saturday morning.

After completing three circuits and his katas, he was drenched in sweat. He took a slow jog back to the condo to cool down followed by a walk to recover. Sonny then went upstairs and showered before scrambling some eggs and eating fruit and a bagel. When he finished washing the dishes, Sonny felt his phone vibrate in his pocket. He took it out and saw that Francine was calling him.

"Good morning, Francine. Awful early on a Saturday for you. What's up?"

"Sonny, I forgot a card I needed to mail when I left the office yesterday afternoon. I thought I would run in quick this morning and grab it before heading out to meet friends for the flea market in Pasadena. When I got to the office, I saw that the front door was unlocked. I can't imagine you forgetting to lock up, so I backed away and called you."

"I'm glad that you did. Stay outside and I will be there in 20-minutes."

Francine did as Sonny asked and watched the office from the parking lot. She made a call and told her friends that she would be delayed but still hoped to meet them in Pasadena, just later than she planned.

Sonny was out of the garage and moving swiftly to the 10 freeway. It was early on a Saturday, so he was able to make good time getting to La Cienega and into West Hollywood. Sonny saw Francine standing outside of the building when he turned into the garage. She came down and met him as he got out of his car.

"I didn't see anything since we spoke on the phone. Nobody left or entered the building," Francine told him.

"Stay several steps behind me just in case," Sonny said.

They proceeded to the second floor using the stairs. Sonny slid his Glock 27 out of the holster and into the low ready position with his right index finger under the slide. He used his shirt to cover the knob while he turned it and pushed the door inward. He scanned the outer area, but nothing looked disturbed. Sonny moved silently to his office in the rear and slowly pushed the door open with his left shoulder. He cleared the room before holstering his weapon and signaling to Francine that it was safe to come inside.

She joined him in his office. Sonny noted that his file cabinet was still locked and appeared to be undisturbed. He unlocked it and did a quick check of each drawer and found nothing amiss. He went over to his desk and checked his computer. It was locked and he signed in and checked his file manager and opened a few random files. All appeared to be in order as he left it. Sonny then turned his attention to the files he left on top of his desk. To the untrained eye, it appeared they were exactly where he left them the night before. However, he was very fastidious about how he placed things on his desk, among other things. It was one of the traits that his ex-wife did not find endearing. She would fold a shirt for him, and he would unfold it and do it again in the perfect way he learned to during recruit training in the Marine Corps. She grew tired of him having to have everything just so.

Sonny could tell immediately that his files had been moved. They were not squared off with the top right corner of the desk which was how he left them. When he looked inside, he found that two pages had been switched in the order he left them in. Sonny knew this because he had jotted notes on each page and left them in the chronological order of his notes. It was close, but not how he left the pages in the file folder.

"They were here and looked at these files," Sonny said.

"How can you tell? Who are they?"

"The two mob thugs from Vegas. They had some of their people rough me up the other night at one of their strip clubs. They either followed me or knew where to find my office. They changed the order of two of the pages, most likely when they left in a hurry. Do me a favor and check your desk area just to be sure nothing was touched out there."

Francine went out to the front and closely examined everything. Nothing appeared to have been touched at all. She went back into Sonny's office and informed him of that.

Sonny was now considering what this meant for the case. They obviously knew that he was making connections between Tony Bianchi's companies and contracts awarded by the City of Los Angeles. He wished that he had locked up his files before leaving but did not anticipate a break-in and was planning to use them again this morning. Water under the bridge now, Sonny thought to himself.

"Should we call the police and report it?"

"We can't really prove that we had a break-in, at least not right now. On Monday, when we can get access to the building camera system, we might have something that would support it, but there is nothing covering this end of the hall. For now, we will put that option to the side. When you get in on Monday, have the building people pull the video from 9 p.m. Friday night until you arrived this morning. We can go through it then if it is worth the effort."

Francine nodded and said she would make a call first thing on Monday morning.

"Do me a favor. Pull up the mayor's public schedule and see if anything is listed for today."

Francine went back to her desk and made the query. "It looks like he has a public event at UCLA in Westwood scheduled for 10 o'clock this morning. Some type of research partnership announcement."

Sonny thought about this in a slightly different way than he did earlier this morning. It now seemed even more important to try to get Lance on board considering recent events.

"I am going to head over to UCLA and see if Lance is at the event with the mayor. I need to look for an opportunity to talk to him. Can you lock up everything when you leave?"

"Will do. Let me know if you need anything else later today," Francine replied.

Sonny thanked her and headed for the door. He would plan his approach to Lance on the ride over to Westwood.

32

Lance stepped outside onto his deck with views of the Pacific Ocean in the distance. He sat down to drink his coffee as the sun began to light up the canyon below. This view was a reminder of why he had to prevail. He worked too hard to reach this point to let it all slip away.

It had now been several days, and Lance had not heard anything new. The PI was not poking around that he could see. Maybe his call to the desert had succeeded in convincing him to go away. He didn't know the details and didn't want to know the details. He just wanted him to stay away and let it drop. The police in Riverside County had not released anything new either. Perhaps the trail was growing cold. Growing further away from him. Lance had been avoiding the condo almost completely and staying in his home in Pacific Palisades, even though he had to fight traffic to do so. Out of sight, out of mind he hoped. If he could just lay low for a few more months, this would all blow over. His little arrangement helped to put him over the top in financing his affluent lifestyle, but he had it coming. He was certain of it. Lance was the one responsible for the mayor's poll numbers. He was the one who had carefully positioned him to be considered for an even larger political stage in the future. Why shouldn't he reap some of the benefits of his hard work?

Lance went back inside and removed a folder from his briefcase and brought it back to the table on the deck. A group of eight pelicans flew overhead, gliding on the wind currents and banking hard back toward the coastline. He pulled out the run of show production notes from the press office for this morning's event at UCLA. This shouldn't take more than an hour, and the mayor had blocked the rest of his day to be with his family. Lance thought this would afford him the opportunity to hit the gym on the way back home from the event. He would take his gym bag along and change at the club. He would drive on Sunset to UCLA and come in the back way. He checked his map application on his phone. Only 18 minutes, it showed.

Lance went back inside the house and grabbed a yogurt to go with his whole grain bread toast topped with peanut butter. He grabbed an energy bar to toss in his gym bag in case he felt hungry after the event. After he showered and got dressed, he stopped to admire himself in the full-length mirror in the bedroom. "You got this," he said to himself out loud. Just keep doing what you do so well, and you will beat this, he thought. Just hang in there a little while longer.

Lance picked up his briefcase and gym bag and walked across the front partially enclosed courtyard and into his garage through the other door. He unplugged his black Porsche Taycan from the charger and got into the driver's seat. The garage door opened, and he backed down his driveway and exited the cul-de-sac, driving downhill on his way to intersect with Sunset. Twenty minutes later, he parked in a spot reserved for members of the mayor's team next to Pauley Pavilion.

33

Sonny headed west on Sunset Boulevard toward UCLA's campus. Traffic was picking up, but he wasn't in a big hurry. He estimated that he would arrive at least 20-minutes before the event was scheduled to begin. The mayor usually kept the audience waiting for a few minutes to demonstrate that he was an important man with lots to do. This seemingly made the audience appreciate him more for gracing them with his presence.

As he drove along with traffic and stopped for almost every red light, his thoughts turned to Lance Frederick. Sonny didn't know if Lance would even be there, as it was a Saturday after all. However, since the mayor was announcing an important public/private partnership that also involved research labs at UCLA, he hoped that Lance would accompany him. The event was scheduled to be held inside Pauley Pavilion, the storied home of UCLA basketball. John Wooden himself was responsible for all the championship banners hanging in the rafters high above the court. Sonny assumed they would use the court as the centerpiece for the mayor to speak from and the space behind him for a backdrop. He assumed there would be chairs set up on the court but hoped that he might be able to hang back and watch from the arena seats. He wanted to go unnoticed by Lance until he figured out how to play it. Sonny had to be careful not to create a stir, as any unwanted attention would negatively impact the interaction that he hoped to have. The best-case scenario would be to find a way to speak privately with Lance out of the view of the attendees after the event concluded. He would just have to assess the layout and make decisions on the fly once he saw the set-up.

After he turned north onto Westwood Plaza from Wilshire, he was almost there. What a tremendous campus, Sonny thought. Every time he visited this place he came away impressed by its beauty. USC seemed to have more notoriety in certain circles, but this campus was a hidden gem. He slowed down as traffic was queued by security adjacent to a parking garage across from the football practice fields. He would park here and walk the short distance over to the pavilion.

As he walked past the conference center to enter Pauley Pavilion at the southeast corner, Sonny observed an area cordoned off with bike rack and several uniformed campus police officers. This was most likely the area they selected to park VIP vehicles for the event. He entered the arena and went through security. They were using metal detectors as he anticipated, so he had made the decision to leave his gun secured inside his car. He went inside the seating area and found the layout close to what he imagined. It looked like they were filling the seats on the court first but were going to permit any overflow to sit in the stadium seats facing the speakers. Sonny took advantage of this and worked his way inconspicuously to a seat that afforded him a good view from an elevated position where he could quickly exit when the event concluded.

As expected, the event did not begin until 10:15 a.m., after the mayor was brought from behind the backdrop to his seat. Sonny looked closely and was elated to see that Lance had emerged from the same spot and drifted off to the right where he could take note of the members of the media that were present. Next to Lance were two others, most likely press staffers from the mayor's office. As the speakers were introduced and gave their remarks, Sonny considered his plan. He could try to approach Lance after the crowd thinned out at the end, but he couldn't be sure how long Lance would mill around the mayor and try to influence the one-on-one stand-up interviews that would no doubt follow the event. Instead, he devised a plan to watch things from his position and then exit before the crowd thinned out too much that he might be noticed. Then he would take up a position outside where he had a view of the VIP parking area. Sonny hoped to spot Lance getting into his vehicle at a distance and then hustle back to the parking garage to jump in his car to follow him. The good news was that campus police were routing traffic out in one direction, and he knew where he would need to go to try and intercept Lance. He had a reasonably good chance of catching up to Lance's vehicle before traffic got too far from campus and began to turn in different directions. Then, he could follow Lance and try to arrange the encounter when he stopped or returned home.

At the conclusion of the event, Sonny watched the security detail maneuver the mayor to the various media members that Lance and the press people had positioned close by for the stand-up interviews. Each local network that was present and in good graces with the administration would be able to bring their viewers a more intimate spin on the event. As Sonny saw these interviews begin to wrap up and some media members head for the exits, the crowd had thinned and a few of the other speakers were posing for photos with the mayor and UCLA administrators. He picked this time to go outside and find his surveillance post.

Sonny was able to find a location near the conference center that afforded him an unobstructed view of the VIP parking area, as close to the parking garage as he could get. He waited another twenty minutes or so before he observed a member of the security team open the back door to the SUV and begin scanning the area for threats while holding onto the door with his right hand. It wouldn't be long now, Sonny thought. A few moments later the mayor was moved from the arena to the vehicle and he and his detail exited the area proceeding in the opposite direction from the rest of the traffic being routed by event security. A few minutes after that, Lance emerged along with several others who then split up and went toward their cars. Sonny saw Lance open the driver side door to a black Porsche EV and immediately headed for the garage and his vehicle.

The only concern Sonny had when he emerged from the garage and approached the road was whether Lance would exit in the same direction that the mayor did. That would blow his whole plan as he didn't have a way to get to the exit point with traffic being directed one way south. Oh well, he would find out soon enough, he thought as he pulled out.

Traffic was flowing and Sonny went around slower cars to try to move up in position. About two blocks north of Wilshire, he saw the Porsche up ahead. It turned west on Wilshire and Sonny followed from his position behind him. Once he turned onto Wilshire, Sonny used the additional traffic lanes to close the distance so that he was far enough back not to be noticed, but close enough not to lose sight of Lance as he continued west and under the 405 freeway. Shortly after that, Lance turned right on San Vincente toward Brentwood. Maybe he was going back home, Sonny thought. That would be fine with him. He could catch him at his home and attempt to speak with him there.

34

Tony Bianchi didn't forge his reputation by being soft. As a young up and coming thug, he became known for his penchant to use violence as a tool whenever it suited his purposes. Sometimes, he chose to use it even when he didn't need to. His rise through the ranks was hastened by the fact that he would not hesitate to carry out the orders of those above him, and always seemed to brutally exceed expectations in doing so. Some guys were message senders, and some were not.

As Tony considered the information that he learned last night about the activities of one Sonny Romano, he knew that he would need to take some sort of action. There were risks associated with acting, but they needed to be weighed against the risks of not doing so. Romano now seemed to suspect that Tony was involved with Lance in a conspiracy to defraud the taxpayers of the City of Los Angeles by rigging the contract bid process. This, in and of itself was a problem, because it could bring unwanted attention and the scrutiny of law enforcement, including the FBI's public corruption unit. First though, they would have to prove that something illegal occurred. He had good lawyers that could greatly reduce the risk of a conviction, or if somehow one occurred, of him doing any significant jail time.

The second issue was more problematic. If the police connected him to Lance and the murder of his nosy girlfriend, Tony would spend the rest of his life in a cell at Pelican Bay. That was not an outcome that he would permit to occur.

The common denominator in both cases was Lance. He could directly link him to both problems if he was ever squeezed by the cops and chose to trade to save himself. He was sure that Lance would squeal at the first application of pressure. He was weak.

Jimmy and Frank were having breakfast at a diner a few blocks south of Sunset Boulevard in Hollywood when Jimmy received a cryptic text message on the burner phone. He got up from the table and walked outside to place the call.

One of Tony's guys answered after three rings. "Got a message for you," he said. "The government package needs to be removed. The other one can wait for now."

"Got it," Jimmy replied, before disconnecting the call.

He walked back inside the diner and Frank looked up at him.

"Let's go. We have something to do." Frank nodded and finished his bacon and the rest of his coffee before tossing some money on the table. They both walked out into the bright late morning sunshine.

35

A short while later, the Porsche turned left and headed toward the Brentwood Country Club. Sonny wondered if Lance was a member of the club. He hung back so he didn't draw the attention of Lance. The Porsche pulled into the parking lot and parked two rows back from the front door. Sonny watched Lance get out and walk back to the trunk and remove a small bag. It didn't appear that he was there to play golf, Sonny thought. Maybe they had a workout facility and he planned to get a workout in before going home.

Lance did not hesitate and quickly entered through the main door before Sonny had the opportunity to park his car. He would now have to wait outside and watch for Lance to reappear. He parked in the third row where he could view both the main entrance and Lance's car. He was about twenty yards away and could easily pick the right time to confront Lance as he was leaving the club and walking to his car.

As Sonny waited, he considered how to go at Lance. He expected to receive more denials up front. He believed he would be able to counter them with facts and some bluffs that were supported by logical reasoning. Lance wasn't going to like it, but he was going to prison, whether he cooperated or not. Sonny would make the case that having the chance at some freedom down the road was far more preferable to dying in prison.

At 12:55 p.m., Lance came back outside of the club. He was now wearing workout attire that appeared to be partially covered in sweat. He was chugging from a water bottle and did not seem to notice Sonny exit his vehicle and cross toward the rear of the vehicle parked next to the Porsche. Just before he reached his car, Lance's expression flashed with recognition and his body language now projected a very defensive posture.

"What are you doing here? I already told you that I don't know the girl and that you have me confused with someone else," Lance proclaimed.

Sonny kept moving forward but did not speak until he was directly in front of Lance.

"I know what happened. I know about the affair. It would be in your best interests to take a seat in my car and hear what I have to say."

"This is complete bullshit! I wasn't involved in any affair with a woman that I don't even know. I don't have time for this, I must get home."

Sonny sized him up. "It is the difference between life without the possibility of parole and getting out to breathe some free air before you die. It's that simple. That is the choice that you face."

Lance did not respond. He just stared at Sonny.

"Get into the car and we can discuss this privately. Then you can decide what you want to do."

Lance hesitated but followed Sonny to his car and got into the passenger seat.

"This is what I can prove," Sonny began. "You were involved in an affair with Sharon Summerlin. You insisted that she keep it quiet. For the most part, she did so. But she wrote messages to her friend about it. On the night that she disappeared, she went to your condo. She was planning to end it with you. You invited her there. But you were in Santa Monica with the mayor and thought that would insulate you from what was going to occur. From what you and your partners in Vegas had planned for her. You previously gave her the key fob to access your floor. I have her on video. She goes upstairs and disappears. Except, two goons that work for your associate, Tony Bianchi, are waiting for her. It seems that you gave them the other key fob, your key fob, for your place. The same key fob that you reported lost the next day. All of this is logged in the condo's access control system. They parked their rental car in the garage and went upstairs before she got there. I have them on video as well. They go to your condo while pulling an empty luggage cart that they took from the garage. Shortly after Sharon arrives, the two goons are on video pushing a much heavier luggage cart to the elevator bank with something large concealed under a blanket that is clearly visible on the cart. They proceed to drive out to Palm Springs where they kill Sharon and leave her to rot in an isolated desert canyon. However, the rental car left some tire impressions at the scene. And then I located that very same rental car at the airport in Las Vegas. And guess what? The tire impressions at the scene of the murder were left by the rental car that was at your condo building the night Sharon was abducted and murdered."

Sonny paused to see if Lance had anything to say for himself. He had a look of bewilderment on his face.

Sonny continued. "You got in bed with the mob and steered construction contracts to Tony Bianchi in return for kickbacks. I have the company information and the contract amounts. Once a forensic audit team gets to work on this information and your bank records, you will be tied to the criminal conduct that led to Sharon's murder. Whether she saw something or overhead something she shouldn't have, you and Tony got together and killed her so your scheme would not be uncovered. So, this is why I am here. You have one chance to go in with me to come clean about everything that you know to the police. Because I am going to take everything that I have to them today. And when that happens, you will ultimately be charged with Sharon's murder just like they will. You have one opportunity to provide truthful testimony against Tony Bianchi and his crew. One chance to get out of prison down the road and not die there like they will. It's your choice, Lance. Now what will it be?"

Lance was still sweating, but Sonny thought it was no longer left over from his workout. The gravity of the evidence tying him to the financial crimes and Sharon's murder had been laid bare right in front of him. His creative manipulation of the facts that he had been telling himself was blown apart and he was left with the reality of the situation that he now found himself in. The situation that he created.

"What do I do?"

"You can come in with me to meet with the police and give them a complete and thorough statement detailing everything concerning Sharon's murder and the rigged contract process. Later, you will have to give truthful testimony in court that helps to convict Tony and his crew for their part in all of this."

"They will have me killed. They're the mob, remember."

"You will serve your prison sentence in a keep away status where you aren't in with the general population. Then, you might be a candidate for the witness protection program should you still be at risk when you finally get out of prison. I know these are not good options, but make no mistake, you are going to be held accountable for your role in her murder either way. This way provides you with something that just might help you survive in prison. This way provides you with hope. The other way does not. It is up to you."

"Okay. I don't really have a choice here. If I don't cooperate, I go to prison for life."

"You do have a choice. You can refuse to cooperate and lawyer up. You can roll the dice and hope that all the direct and circumstantial evidence against you will not result in a jury finding you guilty and sending you away to rot in prison."

"No, I will cooperate with the police. I want to get out of prison at some point and have some time left. I can't believe it has come down to this."

"Sharon didn't deserve what happened to her. Neither did her family. And all of it because of your greed."

Sonny instructed Lance to go straight to his house and get cleaned up.

"I'm going to stay here and make some calls to get things moving with the LAPD. I will pick you up at your house in 30-minutes. Be ready."

Lance nodded that he understood and opened the door to walk to his car. Sonny watched him and wondered if he truly felt any real responsibility or remorse for what he did, or if he was still only focused on himself. On saving himself. He was weighing that thought while he watched Lance's car drive down the road and out of sight.

36

Sonny took out his phone and dialed the number for Tim Patrick at RHD. He called his mobile number because he wasn't sure he would be in the office since it was Saturday afternoon. The call went to voicemail. As Sonny began to leave a message, he saw that Tim was calling him back.

"Tim, hello, it's Sonny. Thanks for calling me back on a Saturday."

"No problem, I'm working this weekend. I was on another call. What's up?"

Sonny brought Tim up to speed on his progress with the case and how it impacted the LAPD.

"I just met with the Mayor's Chief of Staff, Lance Frederick. He was the one having an affair with the victim, Sharon Summerlin. Although she was murdered in the Palm Springs area where her body was found, I believe she was abducted from a condo owned by Lance near LA Live, after he set her up. He wasn't home that night but led her to believe he would be there to meet her. He gave his key fob to two mob hitters from Las Vegas who work for Tony Bianchi. I have them on video in a rental car in the condo garage and using his key fob to access Lance's floor. They were waiting when Sharon arrived, and I believe they overpowered her and somehow incapacitated her. I have them on video pushing what appears to be luggage cart with her body on it concealed under a blanket. They then depart the garage and drive out to Palm Springs and kill her.

However, they left some tire impressions at the murder scene from the car. I was able to locate the rental car at Hertz at McCarran Airport. I just learned from Riverside County that the tire tread comparison of the tire impressions from the scene matches the tires on the rental car that Bianchi's guys were driving."

"That is good work, Sonny. Why do you think she was murdered," Tim asked.

"Because Lance was rigging the contract bid process here in LA to steer projects to Bianchi in exchange for a percentage kickback of each contract. I have the information for the first 18-months of this administration and have identified about $2.3 million in contracts so far that companies either owned by Bianchi or where he is listed as a company officer were awarded the contract. I made a CPRA request and should receive additional information that could cause the amount to increase. My theory is that Sharon either saw or heard something that could have compromised the scheme and Lance and Bianchi decided to eliminate her. I'm sure Lance can confirm the specific reason why she was murdered."

Tim considered what he just heard. "If this can all be tied together, the feds will be very interested in the public corruption angle as well as ensuring that Tony Bianchi goes down for the murder. He is someone they have been trying to nail for years. But first things first. It appears that we have a felony assault/abduction that occurred here in LA. That gives us jurisdiction to get involved. The actual murder is Riverside Sheriff, and the FBI will probably want a crack at the public corruption crimes. How did you get Lance to admit to all of this?"

"He didn't actually admit to every fact, but when I confronted him with the video evidence and some other things, he didn't deny any of it. I convinced him that this was his one opportunity to cooperate and have the chance to taste freedom again later in life rather than die in prison. I'm sure that he will outline his complicity in detail when you take a formal statement from him. I wanted to call you now because he went home to get changed and I am picking him up in about 20-minutes to drive him down to RHD where he will be able to give you guys the statement of his entire involvement, and that of his co-conspirators. It should also be noted that he is very concerned about testifying against his business partners in Las Vegas because he might get whacked."

"Yes, that thought occurred to me as well. We can work with the DA's office to put him on keep away here and can coordinate the same with the Riverside County Sheriff's Office when he moves out there. Did he say anything about wanting an attorney to accompany him for the interview?"

"I told him it was his choice whether he wanted to lawyer up or not. My impression was that he wanted to spill everything and wasn't too concerned about having an attorney with him."

"Okay, we can have an ADA here and document everything on video as well. Let me work on getting an interview room and make some calls to get things moving. When do you think you will arrive here?"

"Saturday afternoon traffic from Pacific Palisades downtown will probably take me 45-minutes after I pick him up. So, I'd say I should get to you by 3 p.m."

"Okay, Sonny. Shoot me a text when you have him and are heading my way."

"Will do. Also, if you get the chance, maybe you could contact Detective Stevens at RCSO to advise him of what we are doing so they can plan ahead. He may want to be present for the interview as well if he can get there in a reasonable amount of time."

"Good idea. Will do. I will see you shortly."

Sonny disconnected and prepared to head to Lance's house to pick him up. Justice for Sharon Summerlin was fast approaching now, he could sense it.

37

Lance's mind was working overtime as he made his way back home. Was there another way out that he wasn't seeing? Or was he completely boxed in like the PI made it seem? The thought of spending even a day in jail was revolting, let alone spending a large portion of his life there. Everyone will abandon him as soon as they find out what he was involved in, he thought. His access to the level of society that he pursued for so long would disintegrate. The mayor, all the people at City Hall, will disown him.

His mind raced back to the problem at hand. He could just run right now. Run to Mexico and make his way to a country without an extradition treaty with the US. It seemed as appealing an option as the one staring him in the face at present. Should he get an attorney and try to fight the charges? Maybe an expensive defense lawyer could convince a jury that he was the true victim here. A victim of manipulation by the mob. He felt threatened and went along with them because he feared for his safety. That might work, he thought. The question was whether he was willing to take the risk and gamble by not cooperating now. The risk that could land him in prison for life without the possibility of parole. That was a very sobering thought.

As these thoughts careened through his mind, he was hardly paying attention to where he was going. His route memory took over and the car did the rest. As he made his way along West Sunset Boulevard, Lance didn't notice the Cadillac sedan parked on an intersecting side street. The Cadillac pulled out shortly after Lance passed by.

Lance arrived home a few minutes later and pulled the car into the garage. In his haste to get inside and shower, he forgot to hit the button on the wall to close the garage door. He went into the house and dropped his bag on the floor in the bedroom before stripping off his clothes and jumping into the shower. Lance tried to wash away the stress he was feeling in the hope of clearing his mind so that he could think straight. He was starting to believe that maybe he should speak to an attorney before talking to the police. At the very least, the attorney might be able to help negotiate the best deal for him with them. This seemed to make the most sense. Lance started to consider well known criminal defense attorneys that he could call on a Saturday that might be willing to assist him.

38

Sonny put the address to Lance's home in the GPS on the large screen. It calculated an 11-minute drive by taking West Sunset to snake his way around Riviera Country Club and into Pacific Palisades. The sun was bright, and the surroundings were pleasing. They did not at all match the situation he was here for. The murder of an innocent woman. At least there would be some closure soon, he thought.

He would be there shortly. Sonny was going over everything about the case in his mind. They just needed to get Lance on video in the interview laying out all the specific facts and additional detail that only he would know. Much of the larger pieces could already be corroborated through surveillance video, access control systems, and witness statements. Sonny was confident in the case but knew that having an involved party flip and cooperate would lock everything down and make it bulletproof, no pun intended.

Sonny needed to be ready in case Lance got cold feet and waffled about cooperating. He would be ready to remind him of the consequences for not doing so.

He also thought about giving Jim Summerlin a quick call to bring him up to speed on what was happening, but quickly dismissed it. He would wait until everything was nailed down with Lance's statement and then inform Jim of where the case stood. Sonny looked forward to briefing Jim that justice was in fact going to occur. That Sharon's killers would be held to account for what they did to her, and to them.

39

Lance stepped out of the shower and quickly dried himself off. He was still focused on potential defense attorneys to call as he walked into the bedroom to finish getting dressed. He never saw the man waiting behind the partially opened door who thrust a stun gun into his right kidney area as he passed by. Jimmy simultaneously discharged the weapon sending 50,000 volts of electricity surging through Lance's body. He was immediately incapacitated, losing control over his muscle functions and fell to the floor landing on his face. Jimmy prepared to give him another shot of juice, if necessary, but Frank was ready to go. He had removed one of the belts from Lance's walk-in closet and quickly worked it under his head and around his neck. Jimmy had his right knee buried in the center of Lance's back as Frank stood above him and drew the belt so tight that it lifted Lance's head a good 12" above the oak wood floor.

Lance felt the burning sensation in his back as the stun gun was pressed hard against him. There was nothing that he could do, and he fell flat to the floor. He felt the heavy pressing in the middle of his back while someone grabbed his hair and lifted his head into the air. Before he knew what was happening, he was gasping for air as he felt the belt tighten around his neck. The pain surged through his eyes as the belt squeezed tighter. Lance fought with all his might to break free.

Frank yanked the belt so tight he thought he may have shattered Lance's windpipe. He held on like he was riding a bull in a rodeo. Within 45-seconds, it was over. Lance's lifeless body lay on the floor at the foot of the bed with what looked like a tourniquet around his neck. His eyes were bulging and wide open, staring straight ahead.

Jimmy sat down on the bed to catch his breath. Frank was breathing heavy as well and walked over to peer out the bedroom window to see if anything looked out of place. There was no screaming, or much noise generated from what had just transpired. Certainly, no noise that could be heard outside the house. When Jimmy caught his breath sufficiently, he turned toward Frank who was leaning against the ornate dresser across from the bed.

"I will go out and get the tarp from the trunk. I'll check to make sure that everything looks the same out front. You wait here. We should be able to clean this up and wrap him in the tarp. We'll get him in the trunk without anyone noticing, since we backed in. Then we will dump him somewhere remote in the desert on the way back to Vegas and burn him up. By the time he is reported as missing, he will be long gone, never to be heard from again," Jimmy said.

"Got it. Since we switched the tags on the car, even if there are any cameras outside on the street, we should be clean."

Jimmy made his way through the living room and across the foyer to the kitchen before turning toward the access door for the garage.

40

Sonny turned right onto the street where Lance's home was located. The GPS showed the home to be located on a cul-de-sac at the end of the street backing up to a canyon that dropped off behind the home. He slowed down as he approached the address and saw that there was a black Cadillac sedan backed into the driveway. Sonny immediately recognized the car and came to an abrupt stop. He backed up and parked several houses away behind a large SUV so his car would be concealed from view. Sonny pulled out his mobile phone and redialed the last number he called.

"Hey Sonny, are you on your way in already?" Tim Patrick asked.

"Tim, I just arrived at Lance's home. There is a black Cadillac sedan backed into his driveway. I recognize the car. It's James Antonelli and Francis Orsini. The two hitters from Vegas who work for Bianchi. They are the ones that killed Sharon. I think they are inside the house and that Lance is in danger. I'm going to try to get inside."

"I can roll two marked units your way. You should wait until back-up arrives."

"I don't think I have enough time to do so, Tim. Send back-up but let them know that I am armed and on site. I am wearing blue jeans and a light blue shirt."

"Be extremely careful, Sonny. Wait before going in if you think that you can. I will text you the ETA of the back-up units as soon as I get it."

"Copy that. I'm going in."

Sonny disconnected the call and put two additional Glock .27 magazines in his left rear pocket before getting out of the car. He slid 4 zip ties into his belt near his left hip. He got out and surveyed the area around him. He unholstered his weapon and concealed it briefly along the side of his right leg. As he scanned the area, he observed a white male across the street using electric hedge trimmers to prune some shrubs. Sonny got his attention before calling out to him.

"Police operation. Go inside the house and stay away from windows," he commanded. The neighbor did as he was instructed, most likely after seeing that Sonny now had his weapon in the lower ready position.

Sonny moved deliberately toward Lance's house, taking advantage of available cover and concealment along the way. He stopped to observe while shielded by the trunk of a large palm tree along the sidewalk in front of the home next to Lance's property. Sonny listened intently to try and hear anything unusual emanating from inside or behind Lance's home. He did not identify anything other than a small aircraft flying above.

Crouching down, Sonny moved away from the protection afforded by the palm tree and worked his way to the 4' stucco wall that formed a perimeter along the front and sides of Lance's property. He stopped to take up a position along the northeast corner of the wall. Sonny remained in a crouched stance and peered above the wall at Lance's home. From this point, he had a clear view of the driveway and part of the north side of the home. There was mature vegetation along the wall on Lance's side partially obscuring his view. The Cadillac was still backed into the driveway and the garage door was closed. Sonny did not see anything moving inside of the windows that he could observe at a distance from his location. An orange tree and what looked like a lemon tree also partially obscured the front of the home, along with shrubs that were planted in beds leading up to and on either side of the front door. It also appeared that there was a courtyard open to the sky above on the other side of the front door. Sonny felt his phone vibrate in his front left pocket and hoped that it was word that the calvary was coming. He didn't have the ability to check it right now.

Sonny considered his tactical options at this moment. The early afternoon sunny conditions would not help him. He could try to enter from the front but would be exposed at points during his approach. Also, he felt that it was more likely that they might be paying closer attention to the front of the home. Sonny decided that his best option was to follow the wall around to the rear of the home and try to approach from the backyard. He knew there was a canyon behind the home and that he could always drop down to get around the wall if he needed to.

Sonny moved forward along the wall with his weapon in front of him ready to engage any threat that appeared. When he reached the approximate midpoint of the home while still on the neighbor's property, he heard what sounded like the garage door start to open and he stopped immediately in his tracks. Sonny reversed course back to his original position at the northeast corner. He was approximately 60' from the garage. He heard a beep and cautiously looked over the wall. Sonny saw Jimmy approaching the rear of the Cadillac with the trunk lid up. At that moment, he sprang up and swung his arms over the wall now pointing his weapon in Jimmy's direction.

"Freeze. Show me your hands. Do it now," Sonny instructed in an authoritative tone. Jimmy was now directly behind the rear of the car but Sonny could not see his hands. A few seconds later, Jimmy dropped down out of view. Sonny moved about 6' to his left so he would not be standing where he was last seen. He also hoped that it might afford him a better sightline if Jimmy went in the same direction using the Cadillac to conceal his movements.

As Sonny rose again, he saw Jimmy pop up near the roof line of the car. This was immediately followed by several shots that struck the wall near him. Sonny returned fire with two two-shot bursts. His rounds struck the Cadillac, shattering the windshield as Jimmy dove to his left toward the driver's side rear corner of the car. Jimmy fired two more shots and Sonny ducked his head below the wall temporarily. When he looked back over, Sonny saw that Jimmy had used these last two rounds to move to a position inside the garage and now appeared to be behind Lance's car crouched down. He caught a glimpse of Jimmy as he dove around the front of the Porsche, between the front of the car and the back wall of the garage.

Sonny now believed that Jimmy was trying to get back inside of the house. He focused his attention on the small window of space that he could see between the driver's side front of the car and the steps leading to the door that went into the house. A few seconds later, Jimmy fired several rounds as he moved quickly toward the steps and reached for the door. Sonny fired two rounds in return and struck Jimmy in the left shoulder and chest. Jimmy went down hard like a sack of potatoes, his large frame landing with his upper torso on the steps and his legs on the garage floor.

Sonny focused on Jimmy to see if he could discern any movement. He continued to cover the body with his front sight in case a threat materialized. At the same time, he tried to scan the front of the home including the front door and windows for any motion. When he didn't detect anything and Jimmy had not moved, Sonny made his way over the wall and quickly closed the ground where he was out in the open and exposed. He entered the garage, stopping behind the Porsche first to listen. He did not want to be surprised by Frank exiting from the kitchen. Sonny didn't hear anything and moved cautiously to where Jimmy was lying on the floor. When he reached him, he checked for a pulse, but Jimmy was DRT. Cop slang for "Dead right there."

Sonny picked up Jimmy's gun and slid it into the rear waistline of his jeans. He stepped over Jimmy's body and listened again for any signs of movement on the other side of the door. Sonny began to slowly turn the doorknob while blading himself sideways and out of the doorway to reduce his silhouette as a target. When the doorknob was turned all the way to the left, he slowly and silently pushed the door open. Sonny stepped inside quietly and cleared the kitchen. He stood still and strained to hear anything from inside the home. Slowly, he moved to the dining room next to the kitchen. Seeing that it was empty, he crossed over to the other side and took a quick peek into the hallway. There was what appeared to be a powder room on the left before the hall opened into a great room or living room area. Sonny cleared the powder room before passing by it and stopped and crouched low as he reached the end of the hall. He knew this next corner could leave him vulnerable from several directions, as separate hallways converged into this open space. Sonny could see floor to ceiling sliding doors across the room on the back of the home that opened onto a deck with a view out to the Pacific.

Sonny peered around the corner to the left and didn't see anything in the hallway. He did the same to the right and saw that the room had large furniture pieces and some art on the side wall. Not seeing any threat that could ambush him from behind, he turned left and slowly crept down the hallway, careful not to make any noise on the hardwood floors. The first room he came to was a study on the left with windows that faced the street. Sonny looked inside and behind the door before moving further down the hall toward what appeared to be the master bedroom. When he was a few feet away from the door, Sonny saw two legs that were not covered by clothing sticking out on the floor. He raised his weapon and moved closer to the doorway. He went inside and swept the room before turning his attention to the master bath straight ahead. Sonny stepped over the body and carefully checked the bathroom. It was still steamy inside. They must have surprised him after he got out of the shower, he thought to himself. He went back to the body. Lance was in a contorted position lying on his stomach with his head bent in an unnatural way. His eyes were open, and it appeared that he had been violently strangled and his neck broken. He checked Lance, keeping an eye on him but using his peripheral vision to watch the doorway. Sonny suspected Frank was somewhere inside the house. He checked for a pulse out of habit but knew he would not find one.

At that moment, he heard something coming from the direction of the living room. Something may have been knocked from a table onto the floor. Sonny sprung to his feet and moved rapidly down the hall that he had just cleared instead of using the other one where he might be at greater risk. When Sonny reached the opening to the great room, he heard two gunshots and felt drywall behind him explode and hit him in the neck and back. He turned in the direction the shots came from and saw Frank was opening the glass door that led to the deck.

"Give it up, Frank. Drop the weapon," he yelled.

Frank opened the sliding glass door with his left hand while crossing the gun in his right hand over his left forearm and wildly firing two more rounds. Sonny hit the ground and crawled behind the sofa to his right. When he looked up, the slider was standing open, and Frank was gone. He quickly moved to the glass and did not see him on the deck. Sonny stepped outside but tried to look between the boards he was standing on to make sure Frank wasn't under the deck with a clear shot up at him. The deck did not have steps that led down to the backyard, so Sonny assumed that Frank had dropped down to the patio area below. He looked over the railing and saw him on the other side of the pool near an outdoor kitchen that appeared to be constructed of brick. Sonny climbed over the railing and dropped down to the patio below. He ran toward the brick structure housing the grill area. At this point, Frank was nearing the back edge of the property where it intersected the canyon. Sonny took aim and exhaled slowly before firing one time. The bullet struck Frank in the right upper back, causing him to bound forward and over the edge of the yard and into the canyon below. Sonny ran to the edge, carefully peering over to see where he landed. He saw that Frank had come to rest about forty feet below in some ice plants growing up the side of the hill. Sonny could see that he was still moving and began to walk toward him while taking an angle that placed him directly behind Frank and out of his field of vision in case he still had the gun and was capable of firing it.

As Sonny proceeded slowly down the hillside, carefully placing his feet while still pointing his weapon toward Frank, he heard a loud voice behind him.

"LAPD. Stop where you are and drop the gun. Put your hands in the air."

Sonny immediately stopped in place and dropped his gun before raising his hands over his head, still facing west toward the ocean. While waiting for the officer coming down behind him, he couldn't help but admire the view of the ocean in the distance.

"I'm Sonny Romano. Tim Patrick from RHD should have told you I was here. The guy down below was shot in the upper back and needs an ambulance."

The uniformed officer didn't respond but instead grabbed his wrists and handcuffed Sonny's arms behind his back. Then he grabbed the mic clipped to the lapel of his uniform and informed the other officers that he had one in custody on the hillside behind the home and needed an ambulance for a gunshot victim on the hillside, as well as an assist in getting the arrested subject removed so he could help the gunshot victim.

Two additional officers appeared and came down the hillside. One removed Sonny while the other two secured Frank's gun and tried to control the bleeding. The ambulance arrived soon after that, and they moved Frank after getting him onto a backboard to carry him back up the hill.

Another radio call went out for the evidence response unit and the coroner.

41

Sonny was standing next to one of the marked units, still handcuffed behind his back when Tim Patrick arrived along with other members of the Robbery Homicide Division. At this point, there were several news choppers overhead and the LAPD had blocked off the entire street. Since it was Saturday, they stood a good chance of finding people at home when conducting the neighborhood canvass.

Sergeant Patrick approached one of the uniformed officers and asked him to uncuff Sonny. He did as he was directed, and Sonny rubbed his wrists to get the blood flow back to normal.

"Thanks for coming," Sonny said. "And for sending the back-up."

"It looks like you had things well in hand by the time they arrived. I think we are going to be owing you the thanks when this is all over."

"Another exciting day in the life of a private investigator. Glad these two aren't so skilled at shooting someone from a distance or we might not be having this conversation."

"Yeah, I guess they mostly excel at the up-close kind of shooting," Tim replied.

Tim then outlined the fact that they would have to handle everything by the book but would not be asking Sonny to do a formal interview at the scene.

"Sonny, obviously, you are not under arrest but we would really appreciate it if you would agree to ride with our folks back to RHD so we could get the formal statements out of the way later this afternoon. Of course, you can have an attorney with you if you choose to."

"Yes, I expected that this was going to turn into a long day. I am happy to ride back with the uniforms and can call my attorney from the car to meet me downtown."

"Thanks. I do appreciate it. I know that you wanted to provide everything that you have so we can work with the RCSO and the FBI to put this case together. I know that was what you were planning when these guys showed up and you called me."

"No problem. I want to try and salvage everything that we can under the circumstances," Sonny replied.

"One thing before you go, and we do the work here at the scene. Would you mind giving me a general overview of what happened? We can lock everything down formally at RHD."

Sonny provided Tim with a high-level overview of what transpired after he hung up the phone with him and began to approach the house. He told him about the neighbor across the street and outlined being shot at first by Jimmy and later by Frank. He told him of finding Lance's body in the bedroom and how he ended up on the hillside with Frank. Tim took some basic notes and thanked Sonny for his help. He also apologized for how many more hours this was going to take.

"I know the drill," Sonny said. "I had hoped to bring Lance in to put these guys in a box, but things turned out far different than I planned."

"Don't worry. I have some of my best investigators out here. We'll be very thorough and try to put forth the strongest case that we can. I will see you back at RHD in a few hours. Have your attorney bring along some food for you."

"Already one step ahead of you. See you later."

The uniformed officer placed Sonny in the rear of the patrol car but didn't handcuff him. Sonny pulled out his phone before buckling the seatbelt. He saw that he received a text from Tim advising him of the ETA of the back-up units. He skipped the other messages and emails for now and searched through his contacts and located the phone number for Lauren Mitchell, his attorney. He didn't need to use her services all that often, but she was a former Deputy DA in the Homicide Unit and was very sharp and well respected by both prosecutors and defense attorneys. He hated to bother her on a Saturday, but what could he do?

Lauren answered her mobile phone and immediately asked Sonny if he was okay, assuming the worst because he was calling her mobile on a weekend. He assured her that he was fine, and that it must not have been his day to punch out. He asked her if she could grab him a sandwich and meet him at RHD. He would explain everything when she got there. She told him she could get there in an hour and he told her to take her time. He was still on the way and the investigators would be at the scene for another two hours at least.

Sonny disconnected the call and looked out the window of the black and white as they made their way downtown. Even though he knew that everything he did back there was in accordance with California law, it was always a good idea to have legal representation when discussing the circumstances surrounding shooting and killing one person and shooting and wounding another. And the guy you were questioning gets murdered in his own home 30-minutes after talking to you by the two guys that you shot. Yes, even though he knew he was on the right side of all of this, he felt better knowing that Lauren would be there to provide her very able assistance. Formalities aside, he wanted the police to know everything that he knew to hopefully hold those remaining, Frank and ultimately Tony Bianchi, accountable for their actions.

Sonny pulled up the app for his streaming TV provider. He set the app to record the 6 o'clock news on the two best local channels. He wanted to know how this was being portrayed on TV since Jim Summerlin might see some of the coverage. Sonny would check that later when he had time after he returned home.

42

Back at the crime scene, the LAPD was conducting a thorough investigation of the deaths of Lance Frederick and James Antonelli, and the shooting of Frank Orsini. This was no small feat as the crime scene stretched from the other side of the street opposite Lance's home to the hillside behind it, and everywhere in between. The evidence team was collecting fingerprint, DNA, and hair and fiber evidence, as well as attempting to recreate the way the shootings occurred. They would attempt to collect bullet slugs that were fired but missed their intended targets. Lasers, videography, still photographs and the like, were some of the techniques being utilized to capture and document what happened both inside and outside of Lance's home. It would take hours to document, photograph, collect and store all the evidence recovered from the scene.

As all of this was occurring, detectives were busy canvassing the neighborhood to speak with potential witnesses and reviewing any surveillance video from the time leading up to and during the events at Lance's home. Sonny was right that the neighbor across the street from Lance would be a good witness. First, he confirmed that Sonny directed him inside for his safety as he was approaching Lance's home. Since Sonny told him to stay away from the windows, he went into his kitchen on the other side of the house and used his iPad to view the images from the Ring doorbell camera on his porch that directly faced Lance's property. He magnified the image and watched what was transpiring in real time. He saw the big man try to shoot Sonny from behind the Cadillac. He witnessed Sonny return fire and later shoot the man when he was inside the garage. Best of all, everything he saw while it was happening was recorded. He was able to download a copy for the detectives.

Another neighbor further up the street was getting the mail from his box by the street and saw the Cadillac arrive and back into the driveway. He saw two large men get out and enter the home through the open garage. Later, he heard gunshots and called 911 to report it. All told, there was a lot of evidence that would confirm the account that Sonny would provide in his formal statement to the detectives. In addition, the shooting recreation inside the house would support the details that Sonny would provide pertaining to his gun battle with Frank.

Tim received an update from the detective at the hospital. It appeared that Frank would survive the shooting and was expected to make a full recovery. However, his condition would preclude an attempt to interview him tonight. They would come back tomorrow and try again. A uniformed officer would stand by outside of the room overnight. Frank would most likely be arraigned on murder charges tomorrow at the hospital.

After Tim debriefed with his team at the scene, he took his lead detective to go back with him to RHD for Sonny's interview, leaving two other detectives to finish up the crime scene.

43

When he arrived at RHD, the officer that transported him walked him in and gave him the choice of waiting in the public lobby until his attorney arrived or coming back to a small interview room inside. Sonny chose the interview room because it would be quiet, and he could avoid whatever drama might be happening out front in the lobby. The officer brought him a cup of coffee before closing the door and leaving him to his thoughts. Sonny went over everything again in his mind from earlier in the afternoon. He felt that his decisions were sound. Obviously, in hindsight, he now wished he had followed Lance back home and waited for him in his driveway instead of making the calls from the country club parking lot. But he couldn't have predicted this outcome and didn't beat himself up too much for it now.

After twenty minutes had passed, there was a knock on the door and Lauren Mitchell stuck her head inside. "Are you ready for me?"

"Lauren, come on in. It is great to see you and again, sorry to have to disrupt your weekend by bringing you into this."

"Sonny, did you forget that I was an ADA working homicides for twenty years? I was on call for two decades. This is not a problem for me. I'm just happy that you were not hurt or worse."

"Yes, I'm glad that the US Marine Corps and the NYPD were better at firearms training than the Las Vegas mob is."

Lauren handed him a bag with a chicken sandwich, apple, and an energy bar that she picked up on the way. She settled in and pulled out a fresh legal pad from the briefcase that she sat next to her on the floor. She asked Sonny to start at the beginning and walk her through everything that led him to today in Pacific Palisades.

Sonny went through everything in chronological order, providing more detail on some items than others. He went into minute detail as he described the events that occurred at Lance's home only 4-hours ago. When he was finished, Lauren had some follow-up questions to ask him. She did so and took detailed notes of Sonny's responses. When she was almost done, there was a knock at the door and Tim Patrick popped his head in and renewed acquaintances with Lauren before asking if they were ready to give his statement.

"We are almost done here. Please give us about five more minutes and we should be ready to go."

"No problem. I'll be back in five," Tim replied as he closed the door.

"Sonny, I'm going to have you go through all of this again without me interrupting you when we get started in there. At the end, I will have some questions for you to be sure and emphasize some key legal points for the record."

"That's why I invited you. It has been a long day, and I don't want to miss anything."

"You will do fine. I just want the record to be crystal clear here so the DA can exonerate you as soon as possible."

Tim Patrick came back and escorted Sonny and Lauren to a much larger room down the hall at RHD. There was a long conference table in the middle of the room. At one end a video camera was pointed at the seat on the opposite end of the table. A videographer stood ready next to the camera. In addition to Sergeant Patrick and his lead detective, a female ADA was present, her notepad and pens on the table in front of her seat. Everyone stood when they entered and introduced themselves. Lauren did not need much of an introduction since she used to be the one sitting on the other side of the table. Everyone took their seats with Sonny at the end of the table in the witness chair and Lauren seated to his immediate left. The lead detective was seated to Sonny's right with Tim and the ADA taking positions to the lead detective's right. All were in the video frame and could be seen and heard if they had comments or questions.

The video was now rolling, and the ADA began by thanking Sonny and Lauren for coming in to provide a formal statement in the matter. She said that she anticipated playing more of an observer role and deferring to the detectives while taking notes and representing the District Attorney's office. When she was finished speaking, Lauren asked if she could make a comment before Sonny began.

"My client, Mr. Romano, has agreed of his own free will to be here today to provide a full and complete statement of the actions he took while conducting a private investigation into the murder of Sharon Summerlin, and culminating in the events that occurred at the home of Mr. Lance Frederick in Pacific Palisades earlier today. Mr. Romano is not under arrest and agrees to provide what he knows to aid the police in conducting their investigation into the crimes that were committed by Mr. Frederick, Mr. James Antonelli, Mr. Francis Orsini, and Mr. Antonio Bianchi." She then turned to Sonny and nodded for him to begin.

Sonny started with being hired by Jim Summerlin to investigate the disappearance of his wife Sharon. He explained that Jim hired him because the police could not really help, since Sharon was an adult and was not initially known to be in any danger. He took them through his actions when her car was discovered at LA Live, and when he learned that her body may have been located out in the desert near Palm Springs. He covered his interactions with the Riverside County Sheriff's Office and Detective Stevens. Sonny detailed how he learned of the Condo near LA Live that Lance owned and the video and access control evidence he discovered there, including video placing Antonelli and Orsini at the scene the night that Sharon was last seen alive, also at the condo. He went into detail concerning how he located the rental car at McCarran Airport and how the RCSO was able to match it to tire impressions they collected at the scene where Sharon's body was found. Sonny outlined the city contract information that he discovered that connected Lance to Tony Bianchi's businesses in Las Vegas, and how he had confronted Lance about everything at the Brentwood Country Club earlier today. He detailed the fact that after initially denying that he knew Sharon, Lance eventually agreed to come in and provide a statement and testimony against Antonelli, Orsini, and their boss, Tony Bianchi, for their parts in the murder of Sharon Summerlin, as well as the contract bid rigging kick-back scheme that they engaged in. Sonny concluded with a detailed description of the events that occurred at Lance's home.

Neither the detectives nor the ADA interrupted Sonny while he provided his narrative. They all took their own notes, even though Sonny's statement was being captured on video. After he finished, the detectives proceeded to ask follow-up questions over the course of the next hour. After a quick bio break and the chance to get another cup of coffee, the detectives continued their questioning of Sonny for another 45-minutes. When they had everything that they wanted, they turned it back over to Lauren in case she had any comments.

"I just have a few questions for my client for the record," she replied.

"Mr. Romano, when you arrived at Mr. Frederick's home today to pick him up and bring him in to give his statement to the police, why did you feel the need to attempt to enter his home rather than waiting for the police to arrive?"

"I immediately recognized the Cadillac parked in the driveway as belonging to Antonelli and Orsini. I had followed them in this same vehicle two days prior in Las Vegas. I knew that they were directly involved in the murder of Sharon Summerlin, and that they both had criminal convictions for crimes of violence. I was concerned that Lance was in danger of serious bodily injury or death at the hands of these two men, and that there was not enough time for me to to wait for the police to arrive."

"When you first came in contact with Mr. Antonelli today at Mr. Frederick's home, I think you stated that you had your weapon out."

"Yes, that's right."

"Did you give him any commands verbally?"

"Yes, I told him stop and put his hands in the air where I could see them."

"Did he comply with your request?"

"No. My view of his hands was blocked by the open trunk lid of the Cadillac."

"If he had complied with your request, what would you have done?"

"I would have approached him cautiously and had him prone out on the driveway so I could secure both his hands and feet with zip ties before searching him for weapons. I would have removed any weapons and then left him there for the police while I moved toward the house."

"You said that Mr. Antonelli did not comply with your request. What did he do instead?"

"He dropped out of sight before firing at me over the roof of the car."

"Did he fire his weapon at you first or did you fire your weapon at him first?"

"He fired at me first and I returned fire."

"When he began shooting at you, were you in fear of serious bodily injury or death?"

"Yes. I was trying to defend myself at that point."

A similar line of questioning was pursued by Lauren concerning Sonny's actions inside of the house after locating the body of Lance Frederick and being shot at by Frank Orsini.

"You stated that you suspected that Mr. Orsini and Mr. Antonelli had just murdered Mr. Frederick inside his bedroom and that Mr. Orsini fired his weapon at you numerous times inside the home. And then you stated that Mr. Orsini was running toward the hillside at the rear of the property. Are you familiar with the 'Fleeing Felon doctrine'?"

"Yes, I am."

Did you believe that if you permitted Mr. Orsini to escape the scene that he would pose a danger to the community?"

"Yes. I believed him to be armed and dangerous, and desperate to escape both me and any police that were responding to the scene. In my opinion, he posed an immediate danger to anyone with whom he might come in contact."

"Thank you, Mr. Romano. I have no further questions of my client."

After leaving the building, they walked to a taco stand a couple of blocks away and sat outside at a table away from anyone else. Sonny got them both some fish tacos, as he was still hungry.

"You did very well back there, especially considering the fact that two people tried to kill you today."

"I know that my actions and intent were pure. I did everything that I could to try to save Lance and confront them without having to use deadly force. They gave me no choice."

"I agree. By the way, do you know any more about Orsini's status?"

"The last I heard he was in stable condition at the hospital with an officer guarding the room. Due to his medical condition, they couldn't attempt an interview today but plan to go back tomorrow morning."

"Do you think he will give them anything?"

"I doubt it. If he did decide to flip on Bianchi, they could probably get to him once he gets transferred over to County. I think he is in a no-win situation, and probably goes to prison and does life."

"I agree with you. These mob guys don't often cooperate, at least not the old school ones. It is worth a try though."

Lauren gave Sonny a ride back to the scene to retrieve his car to go back home. The police still had his weapon, but he hoped to get it back sometime next week if possible. After retrieving his car and saying goodbye to Lauren, he went straight home to Marina del Rey. After taking a long shower, he went straight to bed. He felt like he could sleep for a week.

44

Sal knocked on the door to Tony's private office. "Come in," Tony barked. He looked up at Sal over his reading glasses. "What did you find out?"

Sal went on to explain that he made some calls to their contacts in LA and learned that Jimmy and Frank were able to kill Lance at his home but that the PI killed Jimmy and shot Frank at the scene.

"Looks like Frank is going to make it, but will be facing murder charges soon," Sal reported.

Tony considered this information. Losing Jimmy would hurt, but now with that prick Lance out of the picture, he wouldn't be as worried about being linked to the girl's murder. The contract stuff might be another story, but that didn't concern him like a potential murder rap did. They would toss him in jail and let him rot. He only had to be concerned now with the police or feds trying to flip Frank. Tony didn't think that Frank would turn on him, but you never know for sure until something like this happens. They would be salivating to connect Tony to both the girl's murder and to Lance's murder. He would need to get a message to Frank and be sure that he would stand up and do his time if that was what it came to. Of course, they would make sure that Frank had good lawyers and that if he did go to prison, that his family would be taken care of. Tony turned back and addressed Sal.

"If that piece of shit ex-cop PI thinks he can take out one of my best guys and put another one in the hospital and get away with it, he has another thing coming. I will bide my time with him for now, but he won't survive this, that I can promise you," Tony declared.

Sal nodded. "I hear you, boss. He crossed the line, no doubt about it."

He knew Tony well enough to know that he would stop at nothing to put this guy in the ground. Just as soon as the heat died down and he dealt with the legal issues surrounding all of this. It was only a matter of time.

45

Sonny slept for 12-hours straight. He was exhausted by the time he finally got to sleep. While he normally was awake before dawn, the stress of being hyper-focused for the length of time that he was while trying to stay alive, took a toll on him. When his body felt that it was finally safe to let his guard down, he was out cold. Sonny decided to skip his workout today just to give his body more time to recover.

When he walked into the kitchen, he was famished. He scrambled some eggs, made a whole wheat bagel with peanut butter, and a big bowl of fresh fruit. He ate outside on the balcony.

Sonny opened his iPad and glanced at the LA Times. He found an article about the incident in Pacific Palisades. The deadline for the story did not give them time to dig too deep, so they didn't have many specifics. They stated that the police had not yet released the name of the victims. Sonny thought that the limited reporting would not hold for too long, especially after they learned that the incident involved a member of the mayor's inner circle. It wouldn't take long for someone in the police department to whisper to a reporter they wanted to curry favor with. Once that happened, the flood gates would open.

Sonny picked up the remote and watched the two local channels that he recorded last evening. The coverage on both was limited, but the ABC affiliate had some helicopter footage that they showed. People in LA loved helicopter video. They promised to stay on the story and follow-up on the late news at 11p.m.

He sat back on the sofa and pondered whether he should contact Jim Summerlin today. The lack of details in print or on TV, at least for now, might buy him a little more time. It was doubtful that there would be any kind of press conference today. He was sure if they called one, Tim would give him warning ahead of time. Sonny chose to wait until Monday and try to meet with Jim late in the day. Maybe by then he would have a better handle on where things stood with the case.

Sonny decided to head to the grocery store to pick up some items that he needed. On the way back, he would stop at the fish shop and grab some fresh fish to grill that evening for dinner. In between, maybe he would take a walk up to the Santa Monica Pier and back at a comfortable pace. Today was about recovery, both physically and mentally.

He showered, got dressed, and prepared to leave the house. Sonny felt a little exposed without his Glock, particularly under the circumstances. When he walked outside of his building into the sunshine, he took a big breath of ocean air. He was thankful to be alive.

46

Sonny woke up feeling refreshed on Monday morning. So much so that he went for an early five-mile run before the path along the beach really started to get going. He decided that he would go into the office and do some paperwork today.

On the way into the office, Sonny tuned to a local news station and heard a report stating that the police were expected to release more information on the shooting in Pacific Palisades over the weekend. He wondered what might come out today and if any of it would complicate things at all. Sonny had texted Jim's assistant late last night and she responded first thing today advising that Jim would meet him at his house at 4 p.m. if he could make it then. He told her that he would be there. Sonny really needed to bring Jim up to speed on the events over the weekend. He didn't want him to hear things through the media.

When he arrived at the office, Sonny saw that Francine was already there. He parked next to her car in the garage when he pulled in. When she saw him, she immediately asked if he had been successful in tracking down Lance on Saturday. He explained that he followed him to the country club and confronted him. Then Sonny told her what happened at Lance's home afterward.

"Wait, that was you involved in the shooting they reported on TV?"

"Unfortunately, yes. And the two goons that broke into our office got to him before I arrived to pick him up, and they killed him."

When Francine said that none of that was on the news, he explained that most of the details were being held close by RHD at the moment. Sonny told her that he had been forced to kill one of the mobsters and wound the other one.

"Why did they kill Lance?"

"Probably because Tony Bianchi was concerned that he would cooperate with the police and tie him into the murders and the contract scheme. Now it will be more difficult."

Francine was thinking about the scenarios when Sonny's phone started to vibrate in his pocket. He took it out and saw it was Tim Patrick. He answered while walking back into his office.

"Good morning, Tim."

"Hey Sonny. Glad that I caught you. First, thanks again for allowing us to take your statement for several hours on Saturday. I know you must have been exhausted but it really helped us to jump start the case."

"Don't mention it. Although I did sleep for 12-hours on Saturday night. I feel a lot closer to normal now."

"Good. The reason that I wanted to call right away was that I want to tell you that the DA cleared you. It usually takes a week or so to get a decision on these things, but he knows this entire incident could explode in the press at any minute and wanted to get ahead of it. He called on Saturday, shortly after you left, and asked for a briefing from the team. We did so, including his ADA, and shared copies of the reports that we had to that point and some of the video and witness statements. He reviewed everything that evening, and while we have lots of things at the lab to be processed, none of it really impacts your part of the case. Everything that we found corroborated your statement of how things went down. So, I wanted you to know that right away."

"Much appreciated, Tim. I will let Lauren know that I am clear and can put that part of it behind me. Can you update me on Orsini? Is he willing to cooperate?"

"Unfortunately, he lawyered up and refuses to speak with us. I'm not sure if Bianchi got to him somehow, or if he is trying to weigh his options first."

"I am not surprised. That was what I was afraid of. With Lance and Antonelli out of the picture, the only one that can tie Bianchi to Sharon's abduction and murder is Orsini. Otherwise, while we know he ordered the hit, we can't prove it. Same thing with Lance."

"I'm with you. It won't be easy, but you know the FBI will also be willing to assist us and RCSO in any way possible. And we have charged Orsini with Lance's murder and RCSO is close to filing against him as well for Sharon's. And, we have a meeting later today with the FBI's public corruption unit to begin the discussion on pursuing the bid rigging scheme. Hopefully that will get us to Bianchi as well."

"It might if they can trace the paper. But getting him on that is not the same as taking him down for both murders and putting him away forever."

"Agreed. We will keep grinding and I will keep you in the loop when I can. Also, I almost forgot to tell you that the Chief and DA will be having a press conference later today to release more details as well as the names of those involved, including yours. They got wind that the Times might run a big story tomorrow and they want to preempt them. This will probably blow up with the fact that it touches the mayor's administration with Lance's involvement."

"Thanks for the heads-up. I have a meeting scheduled with Jim Summerlin late this afternoon to catch him up on everything. This will be hard for him."

"I'm sure that it will. One last thing. Keep your head down. Bianchi probably isn't too happy with you given what happened on Saturday."

"Yes, that occurred to me as well. When can I get my Glock back?"

"I will follow-up with the LT after we hang up and will text you what I find out. I will try to put a rush on it."

"Thanks Tim. Let's stay in touch."

They disconnected and Sonny could only think about his meeting with Jim Summerlin later today. He was not looking forward to it.

47

Sonny turned on the TV in his office to try and catch the press conference. It was scheduled to begin at 2 p.m., but it was now ten minutes past the hour, and it had yet to start. It was being held inside at the Hall of Justice. This usually meant that the District Attorney would be taking the lead.

When it began, the DA's press person thanked everyone for coming and introduced the District Attorney, who made some opening remarks before calling on the Police Chief to provide an overview of the incident.

"This past Saturday, the Los Angeles Police Department responded to a private residence in Pacific Palisades after receiving reports of gunshots outside of the home. When officers arrived, they found a male deceased from gunshot wounds inside the garage, as well as the homeowner deceased by strangulation inside his home. Also, police found another male on a hillside behind the home with a gunshot wound to his upper back. The shooting began after one of the men, identified as James Antonelli of Las Vegas, fired upon a licensed private investigator, identified as Paul Romano, of Marina del Rey, outside of the home. Romano returned fire killing Antonelli. Romano then entered the home to check on the welfare of the homeowner, and discovered the body of Lance Frederick, the homeowner, inside his bedroom. Romano was then fired upon, inside the home by a second man, Francis Orsini, also of Las Vegas. Romano pursued Orsini into the back yard. When Orsini attempted to flee from the scene by running toward the hillside behind the property, Romano shot him one time in the upper back, preventing his escape. LAPD officers provided first aid for Orsini, who was then transported to UCLA Santa Monica Medical Center where he was treated for his injuries. Orsini has been subsequently charged with several crimes to include the murder of Mr. Frederick and the attempted murder of Mr. Romano." The Chief then stepped aside and yielded the podium back to the DA.

"While this is an ongoing investigation in many ways, my review of the circumstances pertaining to the actions of Mr. Romano is complete. His use of deadly force was justified in self-defense, and his actions were in accordance with California law. We have time to take a few questions, but please keep in mind that we will not be able to speak to certain aspects of the case due to it being an active investigation. Please raise your hand and the press officer will recognize you."

It appeared to Sonny that everyone had a question. The first one inquired as to why Lance Frederick had been murdered by the two men from Las Vegas inside his home. The DA explained that they could not speak to the motive at this time. Another wanted to know if Lance Frederick was killed in connection with his role as the Mayor's Chief of Staff. Again, the answer was deferred. A third query asked whether Lance Frederick was under investigation by the police for any criminal activity. It went on for about 15-minutes with most of the questions left unanswered at this time due to the ongoing nature of the investigation.

Sonny turned off the TV. He knew that the press would start to run with the chief of staff angle and felt that it wouldn't be too long before they began to investigate the backgrounds of Jimmy and Frank and learned of their connection to organized crime in Las Vegas. He would be sure to read the Times tomorrow morning.

Francine had been standing at the doorway and listening to the press conference. "I don't know if your name being splashed across this case on TV will be good for business, but I bet people will think twice about getting on your bad side in the future."

Sonny smiled and picked up his bag before moving toward the front door. "I will be at Jim Summerlin's house if you need anything. I will probably just go home from there. See you on Wednesday."

"Be careful," Francine said as he closed the door.

48

As Sonny drove to Jim Summerlin's home, he realized why he wasn't looking forward to this meeting. It was because he would have to be the one to provide the harsh reality of where the case stood at this moment, and he felt that Jim would be disappointed. Also, Jim would now come face to face with the name of the person that Sharon was involved with and that would probably serve to further exacerbate his grief by ripping the scab off the wound.

Sonny arrived a few minutes before 4 p.m. and announced himself at the gate. He heard the gate buzz and unlock. Sonny went up the walkway to the front door and Jim opened it before he had to knock.

"Thanks for coming by Sonny."

Sonny stepped inside the home and replied, "First of all, please allow me to apologize that I was not able to meet with you before the press conference that occurred a short time ago. I intended to speak with you privately in person before this new information was released to the public."

"It's okay. It was going to come out at some point anyway. I'm just glad you weren't hurt in the shootout. I guess I should thank you for everything you have done. I regret that you were placed in this kind of danger."

They took a seat at the dining room table. "Part of the job sometimes, I guess. If it is okay with you, I would like to start at the beginning and walk you through everything that I know about Sharon's murder and end with the confrontation last Saturday, where the case is currently, and where I think it will go."

"That is fine, Sonny," Jim said sullenly. Whatever Sonny told him, it would just cause more heartache. But it was something that he had to hear. He needed to know the truth.

Sonny methodically presented all the steps that he took in the case, starting at the very beginning. There were some things that he couldn't share when he was first gathering information in the case, but now he wanted to be completely transparent with Jim. He wanted him to know everything that he knew.

When he finished most of it, he paused before talking about the status of the case and where he saw things going with the investigation in case Jim wanted to ask a question.

Jim had been listening intently to every word. Sonny could tell that it was painful for him, especially the details about Sharon and Lance.

"It sounds like you believe that Sharon went there the night she disappeared to break things off with him. Do you think he knew she was going to be murdered by these people?"

"Yes, I believe Lance knew and was involved in planning everything with Tony Bianchi."

"And you said you believe Bianchi ordered her killed?'

"Yes, I believe Lance must have told Bianchi that Sharon learned something about the bid rigging scheme they were involved with, and a decision was made by them to eliminate her because she could expose their crimes."

"Will Bianchi be charged with Sharon's murder too?"

Sonny knew that this is where things got complicated. "Since Lance and Antonelli are no longer alive, Orsini was charged alone with both Sharon's murder by the Riverside County Sheriff's office, and Lance's murder by the LAPD. My hope had been to bring Lance in that day to provide a detailed statement of his involvement with Tony Bianchi, so Bianchi would be directly linked to Sharon's murder. When Lance was killed, it removed that direct link. Now, we must hope that Orsini will decide to cooperate against his boss, Bianchi, so he can also be charged. Up to now though, he has not been willing to cooperate. It is still possible though, as Orsini is facing life without the possibility of parole."

"Isn't there any other proof that Bianchi ordered Sharon killed? What about all the bid rigging that he was involved in with Lance? Doesn't that help prove it?"

"It helps to prove that there was an ongoing criminal conspiracy involving Bianchi and Lance. But it doesn't prove that he ordered Sharon's murder. At least not yet. The FBI's public corruption unit is coming on board to assist in doing a forensic examination of the city contract awards and Lance's financial records. I'm sure they will also try to get search warrants for the business records that Bianchi may have in Las Vegas. While they might get lucky and find some type of smoking gun in the form of a text message or email, it isn't all that likely. Bianchi has been involved in criminal rackets all his life. He learned from the mistakes he made earlier in his career when he did go to prison. He takes lots of precautions now to distance himself from the actions taken by those around him."

"So, even though you can prove that these men work for Bianchi, and they were the ones that killed Sharon in the desert, that isn't enough to implicate their boss, the one they work for?"

"Unfortunately, without Orsini agreeing to cooperate or the FBI finding something related to Sharon's murder in the bid rigging case, the police can't charge Bianchi with her murder. The investigation is in the early stages, and they will keep trying, but I don't want to give you unrealistic expectations or false hope as it relates to Bianchi being charged with her murder."

"It sounds like you are telling me that this guy is going to get off free and clear. The guy that ordered my wife killed and ruined my life is going to walk away with no consequences whatsoever. Is that what you are telling me?"

"I just want to be honest with you, Jim. It is a possibility that Tony Bianchi is never able to be charged with Sharon's murder. They may get him on the bid rigging case, but even if they do, he won't be looking at much jail time if he is charged and convicted of those lesser crimes."

Jim sat there and stared out the window for a minute or two without speaking, a look of helpless resignation on his face. Sonny broke the silence and told Jim that he would keep him updated on anything he learned regarding the investigation. He told Jim to reach out if he thought of anything else that he wanted to ask.

Jim walked Sonny to the door. "Thank you," was all that he could muster before closing the door behind him. Sonny stepped off the porch and felt awful that he couldn't do something to assuage Jim's grief and despair.

Sonny stopped and grabbed some takeout for dinner on the way home. He wasn't feeling very good about leaving Jim in that condition. He hoped that Frank would decide to make a deal and testify against his boss. He just wasn't counting on it.

After watching the end of the Dodgers game on TV, Sonny decided to check the LA Times website. Sometimes stories would be posted online the night before appearing in the print edition the following morning. He didn't have to look hard as the bold headline announced, "Mayor's Chief of Staff Slain by Reputed Mobsters." The story went on to delve into the backgrounds of Jimmy and Frank as well as their boss, Antonio "Tony" Bianchi. The story also touched upon rumors of the FBI becoming involved in the investigation and alluded to shady dealings by the Mayor's Chief of Staff. Sonny saw that the mayor's office issued a written statement highlighting that they are cooperating with the authorities and will continue to do so. The statement also reminded everyone that the mayor would never tolerate corruption by those charged with serving the citizens of the City of Los Angeles.

Sonny closed the browser and decided to get some sleep. It had been a long day.

49

Wednesday morning was beautiful but warm, and things were beginning to get back to normal for Sonny. He was in the office and eager to make some progress on several new investigations that had come in that he accepted. A little over a month had passed since he was involved in the gunfight with Jimmy and Frank. The press had contacted his office numerous times over that span, even camping out all night on one occasion shortly after his name was connected to the incident. In every instance, Sonny declined to be interviewed citing the ongoing nature of the investigation. Nonetheless, that didn't stop people from calling and coming to the office to try and hire him. He had to screen each request carefully. There had been many more cases that he politely declined to take on when compared to the ones that he accepted.

Francine was on the phone speaking with another one when he walked by her desk to grab a cup of coffee. She mouthed "crazy person" to him as he passed. Who knew. All you had to do in this town was shoot a couple of criminals and everyone wanted to work with you.

Sonny was back at his desk reading over a file when his phone started to vibrate. He checked it and saw it was a call from Tim Patrick.

"Hey Tim, what's going on?"

"Good morning, Sonny. I hope you are doing well. I just wanted to give you an update on the investigations."

"I appreciate you calling to keep me in the loop. What have you got for me?"

Tim went on to explain that much of the forensic reports came back from the crime lab. There was blood evidence on Frank's shirt that matched the victim. They also conclusively linked the pattern on a belt belonging to Lance that was used to strangle him and crush his windpipe.

"That is good news. Has there been any movement on Orsini cooperating?"

"Unfortunately, he still has not moved at all. We had one meeting with his attorney, but it didn't go anywhere. The feeling we have is that Tony got to him and may have underscored how his family would be much better off if he stayed the course. Plus, he is in County now and I'm sure he has concerns about Tony being able to get to him there if he provided any assistance to us."

"That is disappointing but not unexpected. Anything happening with the corruption case and the FBI?"

"The FBI has had some luck finding deposits in accounts that were controlled by Lance that are unaccounted for as to their origin. Everyone believes that Lance was tilting the field and favoring companies controlled by Bianchi, but he played it very close to the vest with his staff and tightly controlled communications. None of the people that worked for him had the complete picture of how the decisions were being made to award these contracts. They are still going through Bianchi's records, so they could still find something more incriminating."

"If I had just delivered Lance, this would all have fallen into place. Sharon's murder and the corruption case. I never should have left him out of my sight that day."

"Sonny, neither you nor anybody else could have known they were going to show up at his house that afternoon. You saw them the day before in Vegas for God's sake."

"Yes, but I suspected that they broke into my office the night before. I only discovered it on that Saturday morning before I tracked down Lance. My instincts told me to move on Lance right away because I felt they suspected I was beginning to make the connections between Lance and Bianchi. I just wish I would have gone back to his home and waited for him. Flipping Lance would have brought justice to everyone involved. I'm starting to believe that Tony will walk away once again."

"Hang in there. Hindsight is always 100% correct. It isn't as easy when you are juggling things in the moment. While you may have thought they suspected you were connecting the dots, you couldn't have predicted they would take out Lance that quickly. Everyone on the investigation is still engaged and looking at all avenues. No one is throwing in the towel on Bianchi yet. Trust me, the feds really want to make a case against him."

"Thanks Tim. Let me know if anything changes. I do appreciate the updates."

"You got it Sonny. Talk soon."

Sonny leaned back in his chair. Tony did not make unforced errors. He doubted that they would be able to pin anything of value on him given the update he just received. And if Frank was worried about his own safety in addition to his family's safety, that didn't bode well for convincing him to cooperate.

Sonny guessed that he should reach out to Jim and give him an update. He hadn't spoken to him in a few weeks and the last conversation left Sonny worried about his mental state. Jim seemed to be depressed. It was certainly understandable given the situation. But when Sonny reflected upon his first interaction with Jim in his office at Sony Pictures, he didn't seem like the same person anymore.

Sonny scrolled through his contacts and called Jim's assistant. When she answered, he asked to speak with Jim. "I'm sorry, Sonny. Jim has taken a leave of absence. He isn't reachable until two weeks from tomorrow."

Sonny thanked her and asked if she could relay a message that he called and if Jim was unavailable, perhaps he could stop to see him when he returned. She said she would make sure he got the message.

After he finished the call, Sonny thought about Jim taking a leave of absence. It did not seem like something he would do given that he was back in the office only a couple of days after Sharon's funeral. On the other hand, Jim was probably still in shock then and maybe everything had now caught up with him in a cumulative sort of way. Maybe Jim took leave to get some professional counseling to lift him out of the depths that he was in. Sonny hoped that was the case.

50

Tony Bianchi was on a roll with no butter, a rip with no tear. He was riding a wave of good fortune that he believed was validation of the decisions he had made and the hard work that he put in to get here. Nobody understood the complexities of running a criminal enterprise while staying one step ahead of the police better than he did. He was used to being the target of police and prosecutors but had learned some essential risk mitigation tactics over the years that were now proving to be very valuable indeed.

Friday afternoon on the Las Vegas strip was beautiful. The temperatures were a little warmer than he liked, but that's why they made HVAC systems, Tony thought to himself as he entered his favorite high-end steakhouse. The maître d' was expecting his arrival and made a big deal of greeting him and escorting him and Sal over to his usual table in the back with a view of the fountain in the center of the room. His attorney, Alphonse Pallone, was already waiting at the table. He jumped up and greeted Tony warmly and said hello to Sal. The men sat down and ordered drinks. They had no use for a menu. The server knew what to order and precisely how Tony wanted his steak prepared.

"Well Al, I hope that you have more good news for me," Tony said.

"Actually, I do. The situation from three months ago at the club will be dismissed later today. It seems the prosecution's main witness had a change of heart and is now unable to identify our guy as the man that he saw pistol whip that poor tourist."

"Well now, that is good news. I do hope the police are able to find the person truly responsible for this horrible crime. I can't have violence in my strip clubs." They all shared a hearty laugh together at that one.

"I have to say, Al, you have been doing a nice job for me of late. I certainly pay you enough to do so, but it is worth noting, nonetheless."

"Yes, well, it takes resources to make things go away."

"Speaking of making things go away, how are we doing with the thing in LA?"

"Our contacts with Frank and his family are paying off. He won't be doing any talking to the feds or anyone else. He realizes that it is in the best interests of his wife and kids to stay the course. And he knows we have friends inside that will be monitoring things for us."

"Excellent. I knew Frank was no rat. He knew the risks. Could just as easily been me in there."

"Yes, he certainly did. And the feds seem very hesitant to charge you on the contract stuff. They don't want to get embarrassed and lose on a minor charge to us in court. I really don't see them moving ahead with what they have."

"Nice work, Al. That is some very good news. That deserves another round for the table." He snapped his fingers, and the waiter came right over. "Another round and bring some fresh burrata and tomatoes while we wait for the steaks," Tony commanded. The waiter nodded and quickly ran off to make it happen.

"Ah yes, it's good to be the king," Tony mused. "Things are finally rolling our way. Revenues are up, and it seems the legal issues are now under control. Maybe I will have the opportunity to address that PI issue soon. I haven't forgotten about him."

"Tony, as your attorney, I must advise to let that go. You just said, everything is moving in the right direction, why take any unnecessary risks?"

"While I appreciate your counsel, Al, nobody takes out two of my best men and walks away still breathing. That prick is going down."

"Let's at least hold off until everything settles, and we can be sure you are completely insulated."

"I will wait for now. But when it happens, I want him to know it was me."

The steaks came out and they all enjoyed the delicious meal. Steak always tasted better when you were on top. After some small talk and finishing up dessert, Al thanked him for lunch but said he had to get back to the office to meet with another client.

"You run along then, Al. But always remember that I am your number one client. After all, none of your other clients will literally cut your balls off and feed them to you if they don't get your full attention." Tony said it without even the slightest indication that he wasn't dead serious.

Al offered some nervous laughter as he pushed in his chair. "You know I always prioritize everything related to your cases. You are my highest priority."

"Nice to hear you say that Al." Tony directed Sal to walk Al out and then bring the car around front so he wouldn't have to stand in the heat too long. He had a few more bites of dessert that he wanted to savor.

During their lunch, another man sat alone at a table next to the wall. He too ordered the steak but didn't eat much. He wasn't very hungry. That wasn't the point.

The man cut a small bite of steak and put it into his mouth. He thought to himself that the nice thing about these expensive steakhouses was that not only did they use high quality beef, but their steak knives were extremely sharp. It was much easier to cut the meat with them.

When he noticed the man to the right stand up and the other one follow him out, he waited about thirty seconds before slowly rising and walking toward the man now seated alone at the table.

Tony was finishing his last bite of the chocolate soufflé that they served to him when he noticed a man he didn't recognize approach his table. When the man stood there and didn't say anything right away, Tony spoke first.

"Who are you? What the fuck do you want?"

The man looked directly into his eyes and said, "How do you live with yourself? How do you even sleep at night?"

"I sleep just fine, asshole. Maybe you don't know who I am. I think you have me confused with someone else. My advice to you is to move along right now before something very bad happens to you." He stared at the man standing before him with a look of utter disgust on his face.

"It already did," replied the man as he released his fingers and allowed gravity to cause the steak knife to drop down into his right hand from its concealed position in his sport coat sleeve. He closed his hand around the handle of the knife and in one motion brought it up in front of him, quickly swinging it from left to right across Tony's neck and cutting his carotid artery in the process. Blood began to spurt out of the right side of Tony's neck uncontrollably as the man rotated his wrist clockwise before plunging the knife deep into Tony's chest. As he did this, he leaned in close to his face and said, "That was for my wife Sharon. I guess you didn't get away with it after all."

Jim held on to the knife for a few seconds more as the life drained from Tony Bianchi. Then he released it and turned and walked slowly toward the front door of the restaurant, the knife still protruding from Tony's chest. Nobody moved, seemingly stunned by what they just witnessed. He stepped outside onto the strip before turning right and walking south on the sidewalk. His sport coat, right hand, face, and the front of his pants were covered with Tony's blood. The crowd of people on the sidewalk parted for him to pass by, perhaps thinking that he was some sort of street performer or something. Jim walked over to a police vehicle that was parked on the street next to the curb with the flashers on. He knocked on the passenger window and startled the officer who was writing something in his notebook. The officer lowered the window. "Were you in an accident?" he asked in an alarmed tone of voice.

"My name is Jim Summerlin. I just killed the man who murdered my wife, Sharon. Back there at the steakhouse."

The officer jumped out of the car while simultaneously calling for back-up using his portable radio. He ran around to Jim and held him there, but Jim offered no resistance at all and just stared straight ahead into the abyss.

51

Sonny was sitting at his desk when Tim Patrick called him on his mobile phone. When Sonny answered, Tim blurted out, "Are you watching this?"

Sonny replied, "Watching what?"

"Turn on CNN right now. I have to go into a meeting but will reach out to you later."

Tim disconnected the call and Sonny turned on the TV in his office and tuned to the channel for CNN. He saw a female reporter broadcasting live from the Las Vegas strip. She was describing the scene of a murder inside a steakhouse on the strip that occurred about an hour earlier. Then he saw a photo appear on the screen of the man who had been killed. It was Tony Bianchi. Sonny couldn't believe it. The reporter referred to him as a reputed organized crime figure in Las Vegas. Then they switched to some interview footage shot earlier with witnesses from the steakhouse. The witnesses described their shock at seeing another man slash the victim with a knife before stabbing him in the chest. The reporter said that the victim was pronounced dead at the scene.

The coverage then shifted to the news anchors in the CNN studio in Atlanta commenting on the incident before bringing in a remote feed of a former FBI agent who provided his take on the crime. Sonny watched the coverage closely, unable to pull away. He couldn't believe that Bianchi was dead, just like that. He certainly didn't expect him to go down in that manner, right on the Las Vegas strip no less.

The anchor then interrupted the retired FBI agent and said they had to go back live to the scene for some breaking news. The first reporter came back on the screen and said that her sources indicated that the man who committed the murder before turning himself in to police a short distance from the scene was identified as James Summerlin, a motion picture executive from Los Angeles.

Sonny dropped the TV remote onto the floor. Did he hear that right? Tim must have been given a heads-up from law enforcement sources before the media got the name. They obviously hadn't made the connection between Jim and Tony Bianchi yet.

He picked up his phone and called Lauren Mitchell. She answered and he asked if she had seen the recent media reporting from Las Vegas.

"I have been in meetings for the past two hours. What's happening?"

"Jim Summerlin apparently just stabbed Tony Bianchi to death inside a steakhouse on the Las Vegas strip."

"What? Are you kidding me? Are you sure that is accurate?"

"I believe that it is. Tim called to alert me to watch CNN. They are saying Jim was arrested after turning himself in near the scene. Lots of witnesses saw it happen in the restaurant."

"Wow. It doesn't seem possible."

"He seemed very depressed the last time I spoke with him. I think he was having trouble dealing with the real possibility that Bianchi was going to skate on everything. That he ordered her murder but was never going to be held accountable for it."

"It sounds like he may have just snapped."

Sonny asked Lauren if she would be willing to represent Jim if he wanted to retain her. She told him that she was accepted to the Bar in Nevada and would represent him if that was what Jim wanted.

"Let me make some quick calls and see what it might take for us to get in to see him in jail. I will call you back as soon as I have more information."

"Okay. Call me as soon as you know something."

52

A little more than 24-hours later, Sonny and Lauren walked out of the Clark County Detention Center in Las Vegas, having spent the last two hours with Jim Summerlin in a secure room where his hands and feet were chained to rings anchored into the concrete floor.

"Well, what were your impressions?" Sonny asked Lauren.

"He seemed lucid but depressed. As if he was resigned to the fact that he had no choice and did what he had to do knowing a life in prison was probably his future."

"He didn't seem to be either proud or ashamed of his actions. I do think that he was more at ease than I recall the last time I was with him. Now that Bianchi has not gotten away with it," Sonny replied.

They got into the rental car for the short drive back to the airport. Sonny asked her for her legal opinion of Jim's chances.

"Well, my first thoughts are that he exhibited premeditation by paying for information on where Bianchi would be on certain days of the week at specific times. That won't help us. On the other hand, he killed him with a steak knife from the restaurant. That tends more to spur of the moment thinking, and I may be able to use it. Maybe he was tracking Bianchi and just wanted to confront him and tell him what he thought of him but became enraged while watching him and something snapped, and he killed him using a weapon within his reach."

"Interesting theory. Maybe you could get a jury to buy into it."

"Well, there will be mental health experts on both sides that will evaluate him. That will go a long way toward determining what we will be able to introduce regarding his mental state at the time of the murder. His demeanor right after he killed him was almost catatonic. The fact that he believed, as we do, that this guy was responsible for ordering his wife's murder will also factor into his state of mind. And it will no doubt engender sympathy from some on the jury."

"While I certainly don't condone murder, I can empathize with him. This entire episode has put him through hell."

They rode for a while in silence, each in their own thoughts.

"Whatever happens, I just want to thank you for agreeing to represent him. There is nobody I would trust with my life in a courtroom more than you."

"Don't mention it, Sonny. Tony Bianchi was a piece of human garbage. In some ways, Jim did the world a favor."

53

The following Monday morning, Sonny was in his office by 9 a.m. after a long, tough workout. He was still trying to come to grips with what happened at the end of last week in Las Vegas. He was sipping his coffee and checking to see if there was any new reporting from the news outlets in Las Vegas about the murder.

The media were now taking a deep dive into the backgrounds of both Tony Bianchi and Jim Summerlin. There was a lengthy story recapping the killing of Sharon Summerlin and the fact that one of Tony's men was currently scheduled to stand trial for her murder. There was another story that highlighted Jim's career in the entertainment industry that tried to draw similarities with other crimes committed by people with ties to Hollywood or to entertainment in general. His attention was diverted when he saw that he was receiving a call from Tim Patrick.

"Morning, Tim."

"Sonny, I apologize for not getting back to you sooner. I have been busy on several investigations since I called you on Friday afternoon."

"I figured you were busy. No need to apologize."

"I guess it looks like we can slow down on our Tony Bianchi work now. So much for us not being able to hold him responsible for those murders. The universe did it for us."

"Yes, it did. I'd be lying if I said that I'm losing any sleep knowing that he is gone. His little reign of terror is over. I'm just struggling with what was left behind. Jim Summerlin lost his wife, his career, and likely his future. He really lost everything."

"He sure did. And all because Tony and Lance wanted to protect their cash flow. Seems like such a waste."

They discussed some additional details pertaining to the other cases before preparing to hang up.

"Sonny, one more thing. You know we go back to the FBI Academy days, and I love you like a brother, but I need to ask you not to bring me any cases for a while. I need to catch up on my other cases. This was the craziest thing I have been involved in during my entire career."

"That makes two of us then. I will try to let you recover for a while, but I can't promise you anything. I seem to attract this stuff."

"Yeah, I think the proper term for you is shit magnet."

Sonny laughed and agreed to call him sometime next week to grab lunch when he was downtown.

After hanging up, Sonny was considering how this entire thing started. Was it when Sharon decided to get involved with Lance? Was it when Jim made the decision to take the top job at Sony? He didn't know what the genesis was that set this chain of events in motion. But one thing he did know was that many lives were permanently impacted by it.

Francine came in while he was pondering these issues. "While you were on the phone with Tim, Nick Parisi called. He asked that you call him back."

Sonny thanked her for the message and dialed Nick's mobile phone.

"Hey Nick, sorry, I was on another call. What's shaking in NYC?"

"Thanks for calling back, Sonny. I wanted you to know that Jimmy passed away this morning. His sons were with him."

Sonny swallowed hard. "I'm very sorry to hear that."

"We all were. Even though you knew it would happen at some point in time, with Jimmy, you never thought it would be this soon."

"Jimmy was one of the good guys who picked everyone else up. He is really going to be missed," Sonny added.

"The irony is that three days ago the decision on his appeal came down. Jimmy won the appeal. At least his family will be reimbursed for the out-of-pocket expenses he had to pay for his treatments."

"Yeah, I guess that is something."

"The department officially ruled that Jimmy will be carried as a line of duty death. He died as a result of the terrorist attacks on 9/11."

"There is nobody more deserving of that honor. Jimmy sacrificed his life for others. Let me know when you have the details of his services. I will be there."

"Thank you, Sonny. I will call as soon as the arrangements are finalized."

Sonny put the phone down and paused to think about his friend Jimmy O'Shea, remembering him as a young man. A man full of life and enthusiasm for the impact that he could have on the lives of others. On the lives of people he didn't even know. Before terrorists crashed planes into buildings in New York City. Before cancer ravaged his body. But he never let cancer dampen his spirit. Jimmy continued to have a positive impact on the lives of others, even after he got sick.

Sonny bowed his head. He prayed that the soul of his friend would be welcomed into heaven. He also prayed for Jimmy's family, that they would find comfort in the Lord during this difficult time. Then he said a prayer for Jim Summerlin. Sonny prayed that no matter how things turned out, that Jim would be able to somehow find peace.

Sonny wiped a tear from his eye and picked his phone back up and dialed.

'Hey Mom, it's Sonny. I'm coming home to spend a week with you soon if that's still okay."

Acknowledgments

I would like to thank the people that assisted and supported me in this endeavor. To Pat, one of my former teachers in high school, for serving as my editor. To Jim, Jack, and Steve for taking the time to review the manuscript for me. To my daughter Rachael for designing the cover for my book. To my daughter Allyson for helping me to format the manuscript. And to my wife Andrea for patiently putting up with me as I worked to get this project across the finish line. I certainly would not have been able to publish it without all your contributions.

About the Author

Jeffrey Miller served as a Pennsylvania State Trooper for more than 24-years, working in various roles including patrol, criminal investigation, drug law enforcement, internal affairs, legislative affairs and policy, and as a Section Commander, Station Commander, and Troop Commander. During the last 5 and ½ years of his career, he was privileged to serve as the 18th Commissioner of the department.

After retiring from the state police, he accepted a position with the National Football League in New York. He worked for the NFL for 8-years, ultimately serving as the Chief Security Officer for the league.

In 2017, he founded *Jeffrey Miller Consulting, LLC,* a security consulting firm in Southern California that he still operates today. (www.jeffreymillerconsulting.com)

In 2018, he accepted an offer to become the first Vice President of Security for the Kansas City Chiefs. He served as a member of the Chiefs organization when the club won Super Bowl Championships following the 2019 and 2022 NFL seasons and continues to work with the Chiefs.

He and his family reside in California.

Made in the USA
Columbia, SC
09 February 2024

cdaa0693-2f6d-4f92-9517-bedfe0a2ce1bR01